AF378350

VOYAGE
OF THE SOUL SEARCHER

Dear Beryl
my ace tennis pal
hope you enjoy
Lisa V
x

Lisa Victoria

VOYAGE
OF THE SOUL SEARCHER

NIGHTINGALE BOOKS

NIGHTINGALE BOOKS

© Copyright 2009
Lisa Victoria

A CIP catalogue record for this title is
available from the British Library

ISBN 978 1 903491 76 8

*Nightingale Books is an imprint of
Pegasus Elliot MacKenzie Publishers Ltd.*
www.pegasuspublishers.com

First Published in 2009

**Nightingale Books
Sheraton House Castle Park
Cambridge England**

Printed & Bound in Great Britain

Dedication

To my Mum, with love

Acknowledgements

Thank you to Richard, Hattie and Lulu, for your smiles and support.

Thank you to Pegasus, for your guidance and patience in the face of my indecisiveness.

And finally, to my family and friends because you, like life, are precious.

PART ONE

Sitting in the back of the family Volvo a little boy clutches his favourite rabbit.

There is laughter. When he opens his mouth, pink toddler lips part to reveal soft white teeth and clean fresh gums. This is a young mouth that has never known fear, never ached with sorrow nor trembled with grief.

Wild hair the colour of rich golden straw tumbles thickly around rosy cheeks. Deep brown eyes glisten with excitement. These are eyes that have never seen hatred, cheeks that have never felt the salty sting of unhappiness.

This is Jason King.

He is indeed a beautiful child.

'That boy,' his father says softly as he starts the engine, 'is the apple of my eye. He fills my soul with joy and makes our lives simply perfect. This is going to be the best holiday ever.' And he twists around in his seat, resting his left arm on the passenger seat before reversing the car down the driveway of their home.

'Have we got everything, Mum?' father says, gently touching the shoulder of his wife who sits in the passenger seat. 'Suitcases? Picnic? I know we've got our bucket and spade and our snorkels because I packed them myself – and you, my little man with the laughing eyes sitting in the back, are going to have the best time ever.

Goodbye house. Goodbye garden. See you again next week. We're on our way to bonnie Scotland. Sea and sand here we come!'

And the father's eyes shine with more love than he once ever believed possible – twinkling through the driver's mirror

– making Jason giggle out loud, body quivering, arms shaking with little boy anticipation. For Jason adores the seaside, loves the wide-open spaces, the feel of warm grainy sand between his toes, the smell of salt and seaweed and the noisy gulls.

And now he's on his way. His journey has begun.

June King fastens her seatbelt before pulling down the vanity mirror and briefly rearranging her hair. 'There, that will have to do. I meant to get it cut but Sandra's on holiday until next week. I expect we'll be on the beach most days if the weather's fine, so I don't suppose it matters much what my hair looks like. I hope I've packed my sunhat.' And she sighs, plaintively, as though remembering something significant that she can't quite bring herself to talk about. 'I'll make an appointment when we get back. There's never enough time to do everything is there, darling?' and she turns to meet her husband's gaze, at the same time stretching her arm behind the passenger seat to tickle the hot, wriggling legs of her precious son.

June still vividly remembers the way she felt when she found out she was expecting a child. At the age of forty-eight she was delighted – overjoyed – thinking herself absolutely complete for the first time in her life.

Jason was to be their adored son and he would want for nothing.

And now, as they set off on the holiday they have been looking forward to ever since Stuart booked it as a surprise for June's birthday last February, he glances across at his wife – the mother of his only son – and he thinks there is nowhere he would rather be than right here, right now.

They are only on the road for a few minutes.

Heading down the avenue, they wait for the lights to turn to green before swinging out onto the main carriageway towards town.

It's going to be another hot one.

The tarmac on the road in front of them dips and ripples like iced water.

Streets are busy.

Tables and chairs have already been set out on the pavement outside cafes, menus tucked behind vases of plastic flowers, multicoloured parasols flapping in the light breeze.

'Stuart, darling, we mustn't forget to buy cream for Jason,' mother says as she takes in the hustle and bustle of the world outside the car, 'the highest factor we can find. I won't let him burn. We shouldn't risk his delicate skin in this sun. My, doesn't everything look beautiful today?'

But the world always looks beautiful to June – because Jason is in it.

The driver of the number forty-three is always telling the school-kids off for swearing, for making too much noise, for fighting.

No respect for anyone anymore, he mouths to the air freshener dangling from the rear view mirror, undoing his top button and gripping the wheel tightly, blood pressure rising like it always does on the school-run.

They need a firm hand, these kids. Need to know when to be quiet. Parents don't seem to give a jot what they get up to. It wasn't like that in my day. Back then we had more respect, didn't go around demolishing bus shelters, ripping litter-bins out of the ground or throwing bricks through old people's windows. What we need is a bloody good war to give these blasted kids something real to occupy their minds with. A war – that's exactly what we need...time to sort out the men from the boys.

The kids are at it again. Thudding fists are punched against grimy windows, rucksacks are hurled the full length of tired, dusty aisles.

It's baking hot in that bus.

The driver wipes sweat from his forehead with the back of his arm. A bluebottle hums and flits, banging its skeletal frame against the windscreen. *Let me out, let me out*, it seems to be saying.

'You and me both,' mutters the driver, tetchily.

And then he looks away from the road.

For a split second he turns to see what all the commotion is at the back of the bus and, in that tiny, unremarkable passing of time; in that miniscule instance when not much could *possibly* happen, he loses control of the wheel and the bus hurtles headlong into an oncoming car on the other side of the carriageway.

There is absolute silence now on the forty-three.

It stands motionless on the wrong side of the road.

A deathly hush shrouds the air whilst those around take it all in. And just when the silence feels as though it might go on forever, people on the outside seem to slowly come alive again – figures begin to run towards the bus from the pavement, hands over their mouths, looks of horror chiselled into their faces.

There are shouts from somewhere nearby.

'Someone call an ambulance!' 'Have you got a mobile phone? Dial 999 will you, please?'

An old lady in a floral skirt with a walking stick looped over her wrist and a pull-along shopping bag stands on the pavement beckoning to a young man who has pulled up by the kerbside in a Mercedes. She is begging him to make the call, tears streaming down her face.

Other vehicles pull up to see what is going on. Children lean out of windows and point, speechless.

All too soon the momentum of life has kicked in again. Birds are singing and an aeroplane flies overhead, leaving a trail in the clear blue sky.

There are muffled shouts from a school playground close by as children run outside to do P.E.

A distant drone of sirens comes closer, becomes more insistent. But it is too late.

The car explodes.

Fire spews across the road, spinning shards of steel skywards, flames singeing the grass on the roadside, a rancid smell of baking tarmac and burning skin spiralling upwards into the cloudless sky.

Jason and his parents are in that car.

They have no need for sun cream anymore.

It is all over very quickly.

Soon all that remains is a smouldering heap of ash and baking hot metal.

Their bodies are still sitting in the burnt out wreckage when the ambulance arrives – blackened faces disfigured, bodies contorted, fleshless – quite stiff.

The school children on the bus no longer throw their school bags at one another. They lie motionless at the back, like a film reel frozen in time, unconsciously unaware of the stench of death that surrounds them.

And even the paramedics have to look away, for they are sickened, unable to face the repulsive sight of the reeking scorched flesh: too hot to touch and yet absolutely cold and lifeless.

But they need not worry.

Stuart and June have pleased the spirits well and they are already lifted to a better place.

Assured of eternal resting places in the Heavenly House, their journey is now complete. All that is left in the burnt out vehicle are their discarded shells, nothing more than empty shrivelled carcasses to fill their graves and give their family something tangible to grieve over.

But Jason's story cannot end so soon, for his voyage has only just begun. He has amassed so little experience of emotion during his short stay on earth, he does not warrant entry to the Heavens just yet.

Instead he is sent back to earth to complete his covenant with the spirits, returning once again as a young boy.

The spirits guide him down carefully for he is a troubled soul and very special.

You must find your own way on the earth even though the pathway will not always be clear.

And when your journey is complete you will know.

Then we shall be expecting you...

PART TWO

The Lytham House Children's Home is a granite giant of a building that has loomed on the edge of the sands for over two hundred years.

From a distance, tall grey walls spire between clouds that billow across the vast waste of dunes with their prickly tall grasses and windswept leafless trees.

Lytham House is Jason's home.

He has lived here since he was three years old – for over five years now – with the other troubled, abandoned or just plain hopeless cases.

But Jason is different.

He can't remember when he first realised it, but he is acutely aware that the others don't want him to belong, so he escapes to the beach whenever he can: to his own special place where time does not exist and every waft of seaborne air fills his soulless lungs with hope and nourishment for some kind of better future.

And, if he can't go to the beach, he watches from his bedroom window, for Jason is a vigilant silent keeper of the waves, a secret voyeur of the spiny grasses that constantly sway amongst the dunes all day and all night, sending clouds of dust skywards and blowing fine, gritty sand over anything that stays still for very long.

The other children call Jason names. They laugh at him as he sits by his window, riveted, absorbed, wishing he could live outside amongst the dunes forever and without the fear he has always known.

The spirits keep a close watch over Jason.

They are in despair when he feels this way.

It is the wrong pathway for a young boy with a troubled soul starting out in life, and he has a long journey ahead.

Miss Lemon is the matron in charge at The Home.

She reminds Jason of the old dog fox that roamed around after dark by the kitchen bins last summer – until the caretaker set his gun on it that is – and Jason often wishes he would do the same to Miss Lemon.

Miss Lemon likes the other children. Especially the boys.

They take it in turn to go to her room in the evening for treats, knocking politely on her door until she murmurs 'come in my dear,' after which follows a silence as the door clicks closed. Sometimes Jason waits and watches from the corridor until Miss Lemon's door slowly opens again and a boy runs out, flushed, padding quickly to his bedroom where he reports back to his friends in inaudible whispers from the privacy of his duvet in the darkness.

Jason cannot imagine what goes on in Miss Lemon's room, but he knows he would never let some strange old woman like *her* near him.

No way.

But there *was* a visitor who came to The Home to see Jason a long time ago. A haunting man with steely grey eyes in a brown sweater who *tried* to give Jason a hug, to get close to him and delve beneath his lonely exterior.

And Jason still pictures it vividly, remembers escaping from that suffocating grasp, screaming frantically, face red and arms flailing, charging wildly down the drive before hiding in one of the huge rancid dustbins loitering by the roadside.

Miss Lemon came for him, footsteps crunching rhythmically on the gravel, silently pulling Jason from the bin, slapping his hot flushed cheeks with her cold sinewy hands and jolting him back up the path.

I don't want anyone to hug me ever again, Jason thought later that same evening as he sat knees to chest, alone in the cellar.

But it was bitterly cold and lonely down there amongst the thick fleecy cobwebs, his only company slants of distant night light that flickered across the chalky damp walls.

Jason closed his eyes and tried to sleep, to block out the hopelessness that was closing in around him. Sucking in giant gasps of air to fill his lungs, he pushed it down inside him, forcing it deeper and deeper. But it was a struggle. 'Breathe,' he whispered faintly in the darkness, 'I've got to breathe real good or they'll win – if I die here they'll have won and I'm not going to let that happen.'

At eight years old, the difference between living and dying was an obvious one to Jason and besides, he knew the rules; there was no point shouting for help, no point crying. Everyone else would be upstairs anyway, too far away to hear him – laughing, watching television, getting ready for bed – and his sobs, if heard, would only have brought him more trouble from Miss Lemon.

By the next morning Jason's eyes itched and ached from the dankness of the basement and in the bright kitchen he was made to sit cross-legged on the deep stone windowsill with the morning sun streaking harshly down on the back of his weary head.

'You should know the punishment by now, Jason King,' Miss Lemon spat, like a kettle boiling dry, buttering a mountain of thick crunchy toast in front of him. 'If you are naughty and have to spend the night in the cellar, you must go without food for twenty-four hours. *Twenty-four hours*, do you hear me, boy?'

She spoke with a certain amount of satisfaction, in short rasping vowels, licking the golden butter carelessly from her fingers. 'Perhaps you will think twice next time before trying to run away…'

Then she turned sharply, placing the toast in the middle of the long kitchen table where the other children were already seated, warm in their knitted cardigans and neatly pressed trousers, enjoying their breakfasts of bacon and eggs.

Jason could only stare at the food longingly, the sun burning his scalp, throat raw and stomach knotted with emptiness, the sight and smell of all that food nearly too much for a broken boy to bear.

'Hungry, King?' asked a tall well-built boy with slanted eyes and dark hair. 'Shame you can't have any. I'll eat yours, shall I? If you're nice to me, I'll save you some scraps for tomorrow.'

Jason remained silent.

Answering back was not an option.

Stefan Barzel was a bully – and a mean one at that.

And Stefan is worshipped, revered, for he is one of the loved children; one of Miss Lemon's special boys – and Jason's roommate.

For Jason, there is no escape from Stefan's ridicule and contempt.

It is Stefan who unleashes the derisive torment of the other children, like a snake charmer working a powerful dark magic, when Jason asks Miss Lemon if he can sing in the local church choir.

Later that same day Stefan stands at the front of the class, baton in hand, conductor in charge.

'Come on then, King. Sing like an angel. You're just like a girl after all; let's hear how good you really are. Let's see if you're as bad at singing as you are at everything else...'

All eyes are on Jason.

He sees the nudges, hears the giggles.

Standing with feet apart, toes curled tightly, he can only stare silently at the other children.

He knows the notes won't come.

He can hardly breathe, for God's sake, let alone sing.

Eventually he flees from the music-room, panic-stricken.

Jason never sings again.

And when Jason shows an aptitude for art it is Stefan who holds up Jason's detailed drawings to the rest of the children in the class, encouraging them to poke fun at the carefully shaded trees and finely detailed gulls soaring high over the pencilled waves that crash and race.

Later, in the privacy of his room Jason rips the pictures into tiny shreds of charcoaled confetti and tosses them carelessly out of the window to be carried away by *his* wind and *his* sea to a far away graveyard.

Stefan enters the room as Jason releases the final shoal of paper into the wind. He sees Jason sitting on the window ledge and smirks. 'I should push you out right now and have done with you.'

Jason watches blankly as the last scraps of paper disappear on the wind.

'Do it then,' he replies quietly, climbing down from the windowsill and facing Stefan, 'and get it over with.'

'Maybe I will, one day. After all, you're nothing but a freak, King!'

And he pushes Jason hard with both hands, sending him to his knees.

'Miss Lemon,' Jason asks meekly the next morning when there is nobody else in the kitchen, 'can I ask you a question?'

'I suppose so boy, but be quick.'

'Well, it's just that … that … well, if I *am* such a freak like everyone says then why don't I look strange, why don't I look different?'

Miss Lemon takes an exaggerated breath and bends down to within inches of Jason's face.

'You,' she says, peering into his eyes, 'are a very evil little boy, Jason King. You have no manners and your behaviour makes you no better than a wild animal. Nobody could *ever* love a child like *you*. There are lots of polite, well-behaved children here and they should *not* have to put up with *you*,' and she prods him in his shoulder with a sharp bony finger before turning and leaving the room.

Jason watches her go, rubbing the top of his arm where she has hurt him.

He still doesn't understand, but he is glad she doesn't love him because she smells of beer and sweat and cheap perfume.

Besides, all that love stuff belongs to Stefan and the others, not Jason.

They can keep it too.

If sleeping in the same room with Stefan isn't punishment enough, sitting next to him in class is impossible at times.

'God strikes down morons like you, King.'

Jason buries his head in his book and pretends to be hard at work.

'Do you hear me, loser? You'd better not mess up today. Annoy Kilpenny again and we'll all be for it. One wrong move and you'll be a goner, *thicko*! Mark my words. You get us into enough trouble with your weird ways.'

But God must know I'm trying, prays Jason, silently. Please God, if you *are* there, let me get the hang of this reading lark…

He looks down at the page expecting divine intervention, but the shapes all flit across it in brightly coloured stripes with no seeming regard for Jason's plea to a saviour he has no reason to believe exists at all.

Clenching his fists, he screws up his face, growling and cursing under his breath. Spits of angry venom bubble across his lips like froth from a bubble machine as he strains to recognise the shapes of the letters like the other children can.

Jason's body is rigid, unyielding, as he tries to make sense of letters, even though they have no beginning, no end, no logic or meaning.

And Maths is no better.

Mental arithmetic makes absolutely no sense at all.

'Jason King, *what* is the sum of twenty-nine and eleven? Quickly now, this is a mental test young man,' demands Mr Kilpenny, clicking his fingers and glaring accusingly at the boy over his plastic framed spectacles.

'Loser,' mutters Stefan, 'get back to counting your boats and birds or whatever it is you do all day.'

The other children snigger and shuffle nervously in their seats.

Jason's eyes begin to roll in his head.

He feels clammy.

They're waiting for me to do something, Jason thinks desperately, and I will. I will do something if they don't shut up.

He closes his eyes and steels himself, tries to imagine the numbers even though they jump around like whirring coloured tops in front of him.

He takes a final deep breath.

'Purple?'

There is a chorus of hysterical laughter.

Jason sees the shoulders heave and shake around him as he sits, defeated, on the hard wooden seat.

His face is pulsing angrily now and, with blood coursing forcefully around his body, a rage surges up like a lit match over petrol. He stands up and roars, mouth stretched wide open like a demonic lion, then he slams his hands down on the desk and thumps it forward into the boy sitting in the row in front, using the weight of his pelvis to push it. The boy crashes to the floor with the desk on top of him, a pitiful scream of pain echoing across the classroom as his innocent body hits the dusty lacquered floorboards.

The other children gasp in unison before becoming sinisterly quiet.

Stiffening in their seats their eyes turn to the teacher.

Even Stefan dares not speak.

Mr Kilpenny says nothing.

He merely walks silently to his desk and opens the drawer where he keeps his metal edged cane…

But this morning begins so well for a change.

At seven o'clock Jason climbs from beneath his faded duvet and pads quietly across the room to the window, being careful not to wake Stefan and get himself a beating.

Staring through the grime, he watches the fire-red sun rise over the sea.

As dawn explodes, the dunes are bathed in a dazzling crescendo of light and dark, fingering trees that beckon Jason outside, as they always do, laden on this November morning with cobweb branches of twinkling silver.

Jason longs to be outside, to feel and smell what he can only barely see, but that would mean more trouble if he was discovered, so he makes do with pressing his face against the damp glass and wiping away the trickling drips of condensation with his fringe.

'Pack your things,' Miss Lemon says sharply at breakfast, a plastic smile fixed on her face. '*They* will be here for you at ten o'clock.'

Jason waits for more words, watching her silently from the kitchen doorway, willing her to tell him where *they* are going to take him.

Biting his lip, his frightened eyes follow her every move, like a desperate puppy waiting for supper, his small body tense with uncertainty, ready to give thanks for any small morsel of information that might steady the pounding in his heart.

But Miss Lemon has no intention of saying anything more to the wretched boy standing in the shadows with hollow, bruised cheeks.

She ignores him, completely indifferent to his fears; for she is glad to be getting rid of him at last.

As long as *they* don't hit like they do here, Jason thinks, skulking upstairs, scratching peeling paint from the banisters on the way and suffering the wrath of Stefan who has overslept and who elbows him hard in the stomach as he races past him down the stairs to breakfast. 'Runt! Why didn't you wake me?'

Runt yourself... Jason wants to say, but the words get no further than the back of his throat.

You don't mess with Stefan Barzel.

He is growing muscles in places you never knew existed and he packs a meaty punch.

He can make your life truly miserable ... especially if your name happens to be Jason King.

And downstairs Miss Lemon carries on cooking breakfast for the loved ones, buttering toast, turning bacon, unconcerned that one little boy is facing the biggest upheaval of his young life so far – and he is completely alone.

PART THREE

Dear Guardian,

I regret to inform you of my decision to permanently exclude Jason from The Lytham House Children's Home. This means that Jason will not be allowed back to this establishment pending a meeting of the Home Discipline Committee. Alternative arrangements for Jason's home and schooling will need to be made...

Jason wriggles to get comfortable on the ripped leather and clenches his small boy fists defiantly.

This heap, he decides, is the scruffiest pile of junk I've ever seen. It's just like a rusty tin can on wheels – which is exactly what Stefan said when he looked out of the sitting room window of The Home earlier the same morning and spotted the battered old car on the driveway – and Stefan, for once in his life, has turned out to be absolutely right.

They head slowly away from the front steps of The Home.

The car may as well be toppling over the edge of the world as far as Jason is concerned because he has lived there for as long as he can remember. It's the first proper trip he has been on, except for that one outing to Church in the back of Miss Lemon's hatchback, when he was held firmly by his fraying collar the whole time and threatened with another night in the cellar if he so much as *dared* to make a noise.

'*You,*' Miss Lemon had hissed angrily in his ear as they sat on the hard pew, 'are the most despicable child we have *ever* had the misfortune to have at The Home. And if you don't behave you will be very, very sorry – believe me.'

And Jason *had* believed Miss Lemon, with her cheap perfume and snakeskin glove clamped tight on his collar.

She was, Jason concluded a long time ago, *just* like her name – sour, dimpled ... and *very* yellow.

Jason wants his rabbit, but it is locked in the boot along with the few clothes and other possessions he has been told to pack.

Pushing his hair away from his eyes, he stares out of the window towards the sea, feeling that awful emptiness when something you have always taken for granted is suddenly snatched away from you and you don't quite know what is going to happen next.

It's going to be all right, Jason chants silently as he rocks in the seat and presses his fingernails into the palms of his hands, *it's got to be, just got to be.* But the growing knot inside him tells him that everything is *not* all right, that everything will be happening right here without him from now on – and Jason does not like that idea one bit.

He won't miss The Home or the people, but he *will* miss the wild sea and the boats and the golden dunes. They are the throbbing, pulsing metronomes that give a predictable constancy to Jason's otherwise meaningless days and nights.

A storm is carried on fleeting clouds.

Jason feels the thudding in his chest that he always feels just before bad weather; he likes watching the angry sea when it froths like a mad galloping warhorse, tossing boats within its frothing symphony, before charging up the sand to battle with the headland.

And right now he longs to be out there, feeling silver spray in his face and the chilled wind pummelling against his cheeks.

There are two other people in the car besides him.

When he is sure he isn't being watched, he glances at the driver out of the corner of his eye.

Looks like he can pack a fair punch, Jason thinks, so he sits tensely, in no hurry to do anything that might get him a beating. Jason's already had enough beatings to last him a lifetime.

The driver of the car sucks noisily on a cigarette. He has a surly expression and a down-turned mouth.

You're just like a dirty old tramp, Jason decides, eyes drawn to writing on the man's brown wrinkled arm. Jason spells it out silently. *Red-hot-lover … Mary.*

Weird, but wherever we're going it can't be worse than here, with the beatings and the teasing and the cellar and the name-calling …and Stefan Barzel

The driver suddenly coughs and startles Jason.

'Miserable little sod.'

'You sound funny – you drunk or something?' the words spew out before Jason realises what he is saying.

'You'll sound funny when I've put my 'and down your cheeky throat and ripped out your goddam tongue.'

'I was only saying.' And Jason turns to look out of the side window.

Perhaps it won't be so different here after all?

And he sits still, silently wondering when he will get something to eat.

There is a woman in the back of the car and her teeth don't fit too well. She clicks and spits every word. Jason looks at her reflection in the car's wing mirror.

She must be a giant or something, he thinks.

Jason can't see the woman very clearly. He can just make out the outline of a rough skinned face and mass of fiery red corkscrews that spring out from her scalp like rockets of twirling fireworks; but she sees him staring at her through the wing mirror and she glares back, screwing up her eyes, lips snarling.

Jason flattens his palms and rubs his hands along his thighs.

You don't frighten me, lady, he decides.

But suddenly Jason *does* feel frightened, he feels like crying because everything is different, happening too fast, and Jason doesn't understand change – he has never known life outside The Home, away from the rigid boundaries of fear and isolation and hatred.

He rubs his eyes dry. Tears are pointless, he knows that much. It's better to clench his fists and remain tight-lipped – keep it all in – except Jason realises that the moment will probably come, it usually does, when he really *has* to explode, to lash out and hit something ... or someone.

He hit Miss Lemon once. It was a full-bodied swing of grim defiance, and Jason's mouth curls up now at the memory of it.

It wasn't his fault.

Not really.

Someone had dropped a drink on the floor in the television room before scuttling out leaving Jason alone at the scene of the crime. Too busy on his hands and knees, desperately wiping away the evidence with his bare hands, trying to soak it into his own flesh if it had been humanely possible, that he didn't notice Miss Lemon sweep into the room like an unwelcome gust of wind.

It were as though she had been waiting for this moment all her life, delighted to have such an opportunity, smiling broadly, whilst hatred rippled through every crease on her face.

Jason stood up meekly, saw the look of loathing in her eyes and acted impulsively, swinging a mighty punch in a moment of panic. It caught her cleanly on the side of her owl-like head, knocking her right off her feet and prompting a fearful gasp from Jason.

Later that day Miss Lemon had beaten Jason with a leather belt across his bare back, her mouth crinkled with amusement at the sweet revenge of each lash, ignoring his little boy screams, pleas of innocence and the sight of his reddened, broken skin.

'You will ... be taught ... a lesson,' she said, each thrash of the belt delivered in perfect rhythm with the mocking sweetness of her tone. 'You ... are evil ... and now ... you will ... be locked ... in the cellar ... with the other ...vermin ... that scuttle ... across ... the dirty ... stone floor ... all night.'

And Jason *was* taught an important lesson ... that the other kids were mean and *could not* understand ... and grown-ups must never be trusted for they *would not* understand.

Happiness and Love were merely indescribable fantasies that occurred in fairy stories, never to knock on the door of Jason King's life.

The car doesn't smell too good – a rancid combination of tobacco and sweat.

Jason feels sick.

He moves to open the window a little.

'Not so fast, you little bugger!'

An arm grabs Jason's wrist tightly and he feels a raw burning sensation on his skin.

'Ouch! Get off!' Jason is big for his age and the driver is only of slight build but, even so, he takes Jason by surprise and there is no way Jason can pull away.

He soon stops trying. A picture of Stefan Barzel flashes into his head like piercing light on a dark day. Stefan used to hurt me like this, he thinks, flesh twisting up his arm in spasm, but this man's even stronger than Stefan.

'Seamus, that kid smells of pee or something,' whines the woman in the back. 'Do they not have baths nor nothin' at that place? He needs a ruddy good wash, dirty pig.'

Jason screws up his face and nods towards the window, hoping Seamus will get the message and let some air into the car.

'Okay, I'll do it,' he roughly lets go of Jason's arm to wind down the window a little, 'don't trust you though – you might leap out – devious little sod.'

Jason's arm is still stinging.

It is red and swollen.

But Jason is used to pain.

Pain doesn't matter.

Outside, the direction of the coastal wind suddenly shifts and a swirling flurry of sand engulfs the car in a blinding storm, rocking it sideways. Jason inhales deeply as tiny particles flutter through the partially open window until Seamus quickly winds it closed again, cursing under his breath, leaving Jason with nothing apart from a light dusting of sand on his lap and the sure knowledge that he is going somewhere with these strange people and he probably isn't coming back.

They can take him away from The Home. He doesn't mind that. But he doesn't want to leave the dunes and the boats and the racing sky.

Jason takes a huge breath in to calm the thumping in his chest, just as the car comes to the end of the gravel road and swings lazily out onto the main road.

The sudden transition to smooth tarmac is a welcome respite. Jason's breathing slows and his head clears. He watches a new world unfold outside his window. The voices in the car stop too and everything becomes peaceful.

Jason's fear subsides, his clenched fists softening of their own accord as the car accelerates powerfully up the hill and past the Lifeboat station, away from The Home … away from the sea. Trying hard to capture a last fleeting glance of the boats on the sea, Jason turns in his seat. But he's too late.

There is nothing now, save the rows of houses and litter-strewn kerbsides and the dusty tarmac road.

He will have to make do with his dreams. He will always have those.

Closing his eyes, Jason strains to count shadows of flapping sails in his head. There are so many boats, hundreds, maybe more – blue and gold and other colours too – all glinting in the flickering sun as they sail away into the distance, to unreachable corners of his mind.

Where are they going?

Jason wants to reach out and touch them. A strange new energy burns within him, an unfamiliar sense of optimism and hope that is beyond his childlike understanding. Surely something with so much colour and energy has to be alive and really happening … it must be … somewhere?

PART FOUR

'Understand good and proper what you done?' drawls Seamus, slicing a knife-edge through the silence. 'Do ya?' He relinquishes his grip on the worn steering wheel, flicking ash from his cigarette onto the carpet before grinding the smouldering heap beneath his feet.

His gaze does not deviate for one second from the road ahead.

It takes Jason a second or two to realise he is being spoken to, but he keeps his head down anyway and says nothing.

Seamus clears his throat and spits onto the carpet next to Jason. Jason swings his legs out of the way just in time and stares at the bubbles of phlegm as they slowly melt away into the fabric of the car.

He screws up his face.

'What's the matter, lad? Too posh to spit?'

'Not allowed,' Jason replies sulkily, staring out of the window, 'Miss Lemon says it's *dirty*.'

'Well, Miss Lemon knows bugger all then, don't Miss Lemon?'

'No swearing either or we'll go to hell when we die.'

'You're goin' that way anyways from what I've 'eard – might as well spit and swear whilst you got the chance.'

'Where are you taking me?'

'Somewheres.'

'Where's that?'

'You ask too many questions.'

In the back of the car Mary is reading a letter from The Home. Blunt words on crisp white paper. She chants them over and over again like an irritating, meaningless mantra.

Be quiet, Jason thinks silently, rubbing his temples with his grubby fingers and leaving dirty marks on the sides of his face, you're making too much noise, just be damn quiet.

'Sorry state,' continues Seamus, 'you don't deserve a good home like what you'll get wi' us. What do *you* think, our Mary?'

'I think this kid must be tapped to do what he's done. We never asked for no criminal to come and live wi' us, did we? Why we've ended up wi' 'im I'll never know. I guess we just got no damn choice what sort of kid they send us these days.'

Satisfied that Mary agrees with him, Seamus turns his attention back to Jason. 'It ain't up to us see, more's the pity. So you best behave whilst you're living under *my* roof, sunshine, or you'll pay for it. I wonder where your Ma and Pa is? Dead and buried probably. Best place, eh? They won't 'ave to live with the shame of what you done.'

Jason feels a lump in his throat, a tightening in his stomach at the mention of his parents.

He still thinks about them from time to time, even though they have no names and he can't remember the shapes of their faces or the sounds of their voices. He does not know where they are, if they really are dead or alive, whether they ever loved him or not.

He assumes they are dead, as Seamus is so quick to point out, but there is no way of really finding out, for who could he ask, who would be interested enough in him to care? Besides, there's no point sharing all this now with Seamus, because Seamus has already made his mind up about Jason.

'It doesn't matter anyway,' Jason mumbles, 'they're not here so that's *that*.'

But he swears silently to himself all the same because it clearly *does* matter, for one fleeting moment it is all that matters in the whole world and it hurts with a searing ache he has never felt before.

'What you sayin'?' bellows Seamus, '… speak proper, lad! I can't stand kids who mutter.'

'I said it doesn't matter and … and it wasn't my fault.' Jason's voice begins to shake so he digs his nails into the palms of his hands in an effort to distract him.

'So who did it then – a ghost? They found you with blood on your hands. Lord knows that's incriminatin' evidence if you asks me.'

Then Seamus sniggers. 'How stupid do you think we is? Suppose you expect Mary and me to believe you is innocent? Just because we're takin' you in don't mean we're 'appy about it. But we get more dosh for a no-hoper like you and times are tough.' He looks through the mirror at Mary. 'Got no choice 'ave we, love? You'll 'ave to get him in at some school or other, eh, our Mary?'

'Ay, suppose so. Will try Leicester Road Juniors – don't know if they'll 'ave him though – wi' him tryin' to kill someone an' all – might scare t'other kiddies away.'

Mary laughs out loud, a raucous cackle, and Jason's anger festers silently like a thorny splinter about to erupt through the skin. It takes everything he has not to turn around in his seat and plant a blow on Mary's face, but he shrugs his shoulders and fights hard to fend off the familiar thudding in his chest, the singular weakness that could push him right over the brink if left unchecked.

Seamus can rant and rave all he wants but I'm not going to tell him anything, he swears silently.

If he wants to know he should ask at The Home – or the hospital – or even the police.

Maybe then he would learn that *nothing* was ever proven.

But Seamus doesn't really care.

He has already decided it is all Jason's fault … just like everybody else.

In truth, Jason can only vaguely remember the night *it* happened six weeks ago.

A Thursday.

Ironing day.

All the children were in their bedrooms, putting away their clean clothes and making their beds before going downstairs for supper.

'I'll have this,' said Stefan, snatching Jason's only decent sweater from his pile of clean laundry.

He held it up against his chest. 'God, it's tatty, but mine's got holes in it. At least this one *looks* newer.'

Jason stared, but said nothing.

He had a vain hope that Stefan would see fit to give him his own threadbare sweater in exchange, but he daren't ask for it. He didn't want another thumping.

'I'm starving. It's ages 'til supper. Go and get me something to eat from the kitchen,' Stefan growled, his back to Jason.

Jason slithered silently out of the room.

There was no point trying to stand up to Stefan.

He'd learnt that a long time ago.

Stefan was in charge of *all* the children and he had a mean temper.

Jason made his way downstairs.

He knew Stefan liked biscuits, especially the half coated chocolate ones Miss Lemon kept for special occasions, and he knew where they were kept. What Jason didn't realise was that the cook was watching him as he sneaked into the kitchen and, a few minutes later, when he was caught red-handed with a fistful of biscuits, all he could think of was the severe beating he would get from Stefan when he found out he wouldn't be getting any biscuits after all. It was a thought that was quickly replaced with unravelling terror when he was made to stand next to the pantry door in the kitchen and wait for Miss Lemon to come downstairs to deliver details of his punishment.

Not the cellar, not the cellar, he chanted silently, blood pulsing desperately through his body, a cold sweat wrapping his clammy flesh in a blanket of dizziness.

And then fear took a strange hold of Jason and overwhelmed his senses; a carving knife was stealthily removed from the draining board next to the kitchen sink and was plunged repeatedly into the cook's shoulder as she chopped carrots and sautéed onions for the evening meal.

By now the other children were downstairs watching a quiz show on the television in the playroom, warm and happy in their pyjamas, sweetly oblivious to what was going on in the kitchen ... until they witnessed for themselves the haunting, piercing screams.

Jason came round seconds later on hearing the spine tingling cry exuding from Miss Lemon's lips when she entered the kitchen and saw fresh blood dripping through his fingers.

'Danger money,' snorts Seamus suddenly, arousing Jason from his daydream, 'that's what I'm gettin'. A kid like you is worth loads more than the normal ones we take in. I'm the only mug who'll 'ave you, see? Suppose it were to be expected tho',' he says, jerking to a halt at traffic lights, ''avin' no parents to keep you on the straight and narrow.'

Jason stares blankly out of the window and sighs. If you are going to get pots of money for looking after me, then I'm going to make sure you earn every last penny, he decides, sinking into his coat, into nothingness and beyond.

Traffic lights turn to green and the sky brightens overhead.

Trees line each side of the road like stooping prison guards and Jason squints as the late autumn sunshine pierces through bare branches, temporarily blinding both him and Seamus with its flashing glare.

I realise this exclusion may well be upsetting for you and your family, but the decision to exclude Jason has not been taken lightly. Jason has been excluded as a result of a serious knife assault on a member of staff...

Mary speaks slowly, struggling with some of the words, spitting each vowel into the back of Jason's neck.

'Ruddy sun,' mutters Seamus, leaning over to fish a pair of sunglasses out of the glove compartment. 'That's better!' He leans back in the drivers' seat and clears his throat once more.

Opening the window, he tosses his cigarette stub out onto the pavement.

Jason inhales the freshness. Trees shush and sway and for that few seconds they are to Jason like the sea. Comforted by their lullaby, he cups a hand protectively over one eye to shield it from the sun and rests his elbow on the windowsill.

He thinks about running away. That would shock them, wouldn't it, but he knows only the Children's Home after all … and the dunes and the sea – and they can't help him now, can they?

Perhaps I can roll out of here like stuntmen do in films on TV, he wonders, half-heartedly, his heart momentarily afloat with thoughts of a renegade defiance. But after looking for a landmark he recognises he realises he has no idea where he is and, instead of jumping, he merely shuffles nervously in his seat, the realisation of his fate hanging in the air like the promise of a rumbling volcano.

'Will 'ave to open your blasted mouth soon,' mutters Seamus impatiently, 'unfinished business, that's worrit is and you'll not get away wi' it, I can tell you. I'm not 'avin' no murdering yob in my 'ouse. I wanna know what 'appened and you're gonna tell me soon enough.'

You have the right to see a copy of Jason's Home and school records. Due to confidentiality restrictions, you will need to notify me in writing if you wish to be supplied with a copy. An official from The Lytham House Children's Home will contact you in due course to provide you with advice and assistance.

Yours sincerely,

Dr. Joseph Gotling BSc. PGD Psych.
Headteacher

Mary gets to the end of the letter.

'Seamus is bein' too nice,' she says, folding it up and smoothing it back into the envelope. And she knees the back of Jason's chair as if to show him. 'People 'ave gone to prison for less than what you done and if it were up to me, I'd 'ave you there before you could shout *murder*. You're nowt but a wild ungrateful animal, that's what you is. I bet your Mum and Dad are glad they be dead and buried. They'd probably *hate* you for all this if they were 'ere.'

Well they're *not* here are they, thinks Jason, so they can't *hate* me, can they? Shut up and leave me alone, you stupid cow.

But fighting thoughts alone cannot prevent tears from welling up at the back of Jason's eyes at the mention of his parents and he is engulfed by an increasingly familiar despondency.

For a fleeting moment he needs someone to say something reassuring, to make it all right – like a mother might – but all he has is this rambling witch with her foul words and nasty mind.

Jason can see her face through the wing mirror. He has only known her for five minutes, yet already they share a mutual contempt.

'Needs more than a firm 'and this lad does. Mark my words, Seamus.'

Mary, it seems, knows a lot about children.

'Well, he can't stay dumb forever,' replies Seamus confidently, as though Jason isn't even there, 'I'll not put up wi' it.' He nods towards Jason. 'Hear me, lad? Do ya? I ain't 'aving no weirdo in my house. You're gonna have to come clean if you want us to sort you out. Gonna 'ave to tell us what 'appened.'

So Jason makes a decision.

He speaks not one more word to his guardians.

For six years.

PART FIVE

Jason turns eleven in July1981.

But there is nothing to set it apart from any other day, no trip to the cinema with friends, no birthday cards squashed on the mantelpiece between pot plants and photographs to waft onto the floor every time the door is opened, no cake with candles – in fact no mention whatsoever that this day is special.

At breakfast, Seamus is in his usual foul mood, eating his toast noisily, mouth open, scowling across the kitchen table and muttering something about Jason ''avin' better keep out of trouble … or else', before roughly gathering up the racing paper which lies scattered over the breakfast bowls.

He stands up, pushes his chair from the table with an ear-wrenching screech across the flagged floor, and glares at Jason's screwed up face.

'Gorra problem?'

Jason shakes his head. The last thing he wants is a beating today of all days. He leans across for the last piece of toast.

'Ha! Too late, sunshine.' Seamus launches himself across the table, grabs the toast and crams it into his mouth before turning to leave, giving the door a mighty slam behind him as he goes.

Jason has to make do with the crusts piled in the corner of Seamus' plate, pushing his sleeves up and over his elbows in between mouthfuls. But Jason is used to making do.

Even his school sweater is noticeably too small, wool frayed, hem ripped, but it's not likely Mary will do anything about it.

It's July, but there's still an unseasonal nip in the air – a fire burns in the grate – but Mary never remembers to keep it evenly stoked and the kitchen temperature fluctuates between tropical and arctic. As usual, she is too distracted by Rory and Beth to remember Jason even exists, let alone notice that he has aged another year and is in desperate need of some new clothes. Motherhood does not come naturally to Mary.

Jason watches her as she feeds the twins, impatiently smearing mouthfuls of sloppy cereal near their reluctant mouths as though she's plastering a wall.

'Eat it, you stupid brats,' she grumbles, forcing the spoon between resistant teeth. Jason notices her hands quivering, sees how tense her body is as she stands up to stub her cigarette on the hearth before tossing it into the fading embers. Another cigarette is pulled from her apron pocket and she emits a heavy sigh, leaning across the stove to shakily light it from the gas ring.

Red corkscrew curls are perilously close to the rising flames.

Jason wishes.

But Mary moves her hair out of the way just in time.

Only when she has taken the first draw does she sit back down again on the kitchen chair next to the twins with an air of fulfilled calm as she feeds Rory another spoonful of stodgy mush.

It is just over two years ago since Mary visited the doctor complaining of recurring indigestion that left her feeling bloated and sickly. She delayed making the appointment for some months, blaming her discomfort on Jason, putting the nagging pain down to the stress of looking after *that blasted kid*. Returning home from the consultation, Jason remembers Mary pouring a large brandy from the bottle she was saving for Christmas, then slumping prostrate on the settee, a damp towel draped across her pink veined forehead.

She lay there contorted and overcome for some time – writhing and moaning like a pantomime dame – brandishing an appointment card for the antenatal clinic and a tiny black and white photograph of two perfectly formed little beings growing inside her.

She hadn't realised she was expecting one baby … let alone two.

To begin with, Seamus was over the moon. He scoured the second hand shops for prams, highchairs, anything that might come in useful that he could pick up cheaply.

'I'm gonna be a real good daddy to these kiddies,' he would say, 'they're gonna turn out proper champion.'

But when the babies arrived, with their screaming, raucous nocturnal habits, Seamus took to spending more and more time in the pub, often returning home long after closing time, drunk and violent, no use to anybody.

Jason stares at the two greedy infants yelling at Mary, banging their fat fists on the table, demanding their breakfast, and he smiles.

Rory and Beth are barely one year old and they are already running circles around their short-tempered, foul-mouthed mother.

Jason really doesn't mind the mischievous toddlers so very much. They give Mary the run around and leave Jason free to do his own thing.

I suppose we make a good team, you two and I, he thinks absently, watching them suck dripping cereal from their chubby fists. You distract the old witch and she doesn't have time to yell at me like she used to.

But I feel really sorry for you – you're related to *them*, you're a part of *them* – and you can't ever change that.

At least you'll be going to school one day, away from the nagging cow and her dirty polyester aprons, nicotine teeth and axe-man fist.

Jason's school is only ten minutes walk from Furnace Street.

He still remembers his first day, just over three years ago, when Mary frogmarched him to the gates and left him to find his own way to the classroom, accompanied only by a stale cheese sandwich and a dreadful reputation.

The other children glared at him as he waited for the teacher by the classroom door, in second hand clothes and wearing a despondent third-hand smile.

It can't be as bad as The Home, he had pleaded silently to the heavens that day, squirming from one foot to the other, please let it be better than *there*.

But Jason soon discovered that children are the same wherever you go, and the children at Leicester Road Juniors were really not much different from the ones he left behind at The Home.

And so, the inescapable downward spiral of Jason's solitary existence, borne of misunderstanding and rejection, continues to plummet him hopelessly between home and school. Eventually all that remains is just a vague scrap of dwindling optimism that one day he might see his sea, and his precious boats, and that everything will work out just fine.

Soon after his eleventh birthday Jason waves good riddance to junior school.

It's a decent present in itself and the only one he's likely to receive.

Reluctantly, Mary buys him a pair of grey school trousers from the charity shop in town, together with a dodgy looking plum coloured blazer with St Cuthbert's coat of arms embroidered in grey and blue on the chest pocket.

Jason screws his face up as he flaps about the sitting room looking like a giant dried prune, anticipating his first day at high school like a condemned man might look forward to the gallows.

'You'll grow into it,' Mary mutters carelessly, taking a long draw from her cigarette.

Jason thrusts his hands onto his hips and delivers a mean pout.

'Quit your complainin'. I'll 'av' you know that uniform cost good money, it did, so give over sulkin' and make sure you get the wear out o' it, you ungrateful little sod.'

September arrives too quickly.

The high school is within walking distance of Furnace Street – or a short bus journey if Seamus has a win on the horses and is feeling unusually charitable. Which isn't often.

A long, low modern building with unpainted walls, it has small square windows that keep out the sunlight and an overriding stench of toilets and stale disinfectant that floats effortlessly along every corridor and into every classroom.

For the first few months Jason is assessed by every expert the school can persuade to attend.

They have never admitted a boy before who can't, or won't, speak. Their embarrassed frustration at his unwillingness to cooperate with them makes Jason even more determined to keep up his silent vigil.

And Jason has another theory too – if he doesn't talk; doesn't let them know what he is thinking, doesn't answer questions in class, then they will have no reason to laugh at him, to ridicule his vulnerability like they did at The Home.

Three weeks into the autumn term, Seamus is summoned to the head teacher's office.

In the morning he comes downstairs into the kitchen dressed in his only suit and a tie covered with cartoon penguins and stale food. He carries a fake air of civilised concern, like some unscrupulous pillar of the community.

'Who's died?' asks Mary as she pours boiling water from the kettle into the teapot.

'*You*, if you don't watch your mouth.

And *you* can 'old your tongue, too,' Seamus adds sardonically, pointing at Jason, his mouth twitching at either side at the sight of the wide-eyed mute boy.

Mary chuckles. 'Who d'ya think you are then, in your posh suit … Jesus or summat? You ain't no miracle worker you know, that lad's as dumb as they come, 'e'll never talk to no-one.'

'Aye, you might be right, but I'd better show willin' and go see what they 'ave to say.'

Later that morning the head teacher smiles disparagingly at Seamus from behind thick lenses, taps a pen lid on the shiny polished desk, and sighs with apathetic disdain. 'We feel Jason would benefit from some professional psychological assistance,' he declares, an unwavering air of impatience furrowed across his cold unyielding features. 'We have a lady in mind who we believe would be *perfect.*'

Seamus nods ingratiatingly .'Aye, sir, thank you, sir, some sort of mentor is *just* what that poor lad needs, sir – it will be good for him … you'll see.'

'What do you know about *mentors*? She'll be more like a ruddy babysitter; won't last two minutes with that little devious sod,' Mary snorts when Seamus tells her about it later the same evening. 'All that dumb fool needs is a good thrashing every now and again to keep 'im on the straight and narrow.'

And Mary is right in one way.

The lady in the cream suit, high heels and ruby red lipstick lasts only four weeks, despite Seamus' desperate protestations to the head teacher that any *-ologist* is better than no *-ologist* and that Jason needs '*summat* if he's not gonna turn out totally bad.'

'It all comes down to funding, I'm afraid,' says the head teacher vacantly, wondering if apple crumble is on the menu again today, wishing Seamus would stop pleading and leave so he can open the windows and spray some air freshener around the office.

After the departure of the psychologist, Jason reverts to his old ways. Alone and unsupervised, with nobody to defend or protect him, he quickly becomes an easy target in the yard for boys who have nothing better to do than taunt and bully.

'Hey, head banger, get back to the funny farm where you belong.

Isn't it time for your nurse to put you back on your lead, Dumbo?'

'Moron! You're a nutter, King.'

Jason fights hard to stay calm, but the old rage starts to eat away at him when he sees their sneering lips. Older boys, heavy muscled nearly men that remind him of Stefan, goading, teasing, thinking it's clever to hunt out the weakest, the most vulnerable. Jason wretches at the smell of their stale breath on his face. Then his heart races, pounds with a solid drumbeat like it always does, fists curled tight in abject readiness, the anticipation of a fight bubbling like a glorious undercurrent, swirling and soaring until it smothers his whole body and mind.

Eventually, powerless to resist and tortured to seeing it through to its conclusion, Jason takes them on one at a time; becomes their mute punch bag, a substitute for the leather football they kick between them when there's nothing better to do.

At last, when the torment is finally over, Jason sinks to his knees, hands locked in front of his reddened face, breathing clogged and ragged. That's when reality starts to blur and he cannot decide whether he wants to live or die; when grotesque images of Stefan Barzel burst into his head, scorching flames burning through him, like a pan of milk boiling over.

Stefan, that bitter enemy, who still laughs at him in his dreams with the same snide contempt that simmers in the eyes of these boys now, arms folded, fingers pointing, always blaming, provoking ... willing Jason to *hate*.

And all the spirits can do is look on in despair... and weep.

Standing in the yard one morning before the start of school, Jason rubs the bruised knuckles he got from yesterday's beating, watches the hordes of boys and girls standing in groups, laughing, chatting, kicking footballs.

The air is cold and damp, angry clouds swarm across the sky in mottled flocks of grey and black.

I'm not staying in this dump today, he decides – no way – and he checks, briefly, making sure there aren't any teachers looking before throwing his bag over the railings onto the pavement beyond and squeezing through a gap after it.

That's how it starts.

The thieving.

After a few days some other boys join him. He doesn't ask them to – he doesn't speak at all – the first he knows is when he turns around and discovers three boys from his class, bags slung over their shoulders, hands in pockets, grinning at him. He offers them a vague smile and a curt nod in return, briefly irritated by their presence, unsure of their motives for accompanying him.

They spend the day together shoplifting on the main street.

The following week they venture further afield, wandering around the new housing developments, looking for things that other people have left outside, for people are careless with bikes and spades and neatly rolled up hosepipes with price tags still attached.

And it is now that Jason starts to feel in control, purposeful, accepted, for the first time in his life.

In the afternoons he walks home with his new allies, always taking the same predictable route, always at the same time.

Sneaking across the railway cutting leading onto the viaduct above the old lodge, Jason always hangs back so he can listen to the seagulls screeching and hear the water lapping gently up on the gravely shore where fishermen rest on their makeshift chairs under faded umbrellas. The others cannot be expected to understand for they do not know what goes on in Jason's unspoken world, so the secret remains his own. But *he* remembers, he feels … though he cannot yet understand.

Running along the disused railway line, out of sight of the men perched silently along the bank of the lodge, Jason throws a brick or two over the hedge into the water. They land with mighty *splodges*, scattering birds and fish and breaking the afternoon silence.

'Oi! You little bugger,' a voice echoes across the lodge. 'Who the *hell* did that?'

'This is private! Get lost or we'll phone the police!'

Jason laughs quietly as he catches up with the others and together they shin over a garden wall onto Weavers Lane.

Sprinting across the new estate of detached houses with scissor perfect lawns, they end up on streets of tiny terraced homes that fan away from the old red-bricked factories in the town.

Eventually they reach Furnace Street.

'Oi! – Jase, we're goin' down Railway Street. You comin'?'

Jason nods before pushing open the front door to number twenty-five. Throwing down his bag in the tiny dimly lit hallway, he takes the stairs two at a time and changes out of his uniform into jeans and a sweatshirt, grabbing his bomber jacket from the coat rail on the way out.

'Oi! You better not 'ave' bunked off again, you miserable little sod...' comes a faint voice from the kitchen.

Jason slams the front door shut behind him.

He barely acknowledges the existence of his guardians and they him.

It works. Their mutual contempt is a silent understanding that appeals to both parties.

It's never difficult to find entertainment on Railway Street.

Too many shiny bikes left in front gardens, clothes on washing lines, stray bricks begging to be thrown through windows or tossed into neat little flowerbeds.

The clumsy naivety of old people who can't run fast anymore and who still remember the good old days when you could leave your front doors ajar without fear of being burgled ... they are all rich pickings for Jason's growing gang.

Today Jason is there with Tom Gething and two other boys from school.

They stand by the gate of a small semi, peering up and down the street to see if anyone is looking. The street is empty, no noise except somebody singing along to a song on a radio blaring out from a room somewhere at the back of the house.

'Go on,' snorts one of the boys looking straight at Jason, daring him to go in.

Never one to refuse, Jason zips up his bomber jacket and vaults cleanly over the garden wall before glancing quickly over his shoulder to check the coast is still clear. Swaggering arrogantly up the path into the house, he turns briefly to laugh and stick two fingers up at Tom and the others before disappearing through the door and out of sight.

Minutes later he returns, jubilantly.

He is carrying a small cassette player and a silver chrome toaster under his arm.

The radio is still playing somewhere in the distance, but nobody is singing along to it anymore. Jason's right hand is bruised and swollen, knuckles raw. The other boys see, but say nothing. How he acquires his treasure is of no concern to them.

'Bingo!' shouts Tom. 'Too easy, but come on ... let's get out of here before we get caught...'

When Seamus arrives home from the pub later that evening he is in a foul mood.

Staggering along the upstairs landing, the boards crackle and creak under his swaying weight as he tries not to make any noise.

Muffled music leaks from Jason's room.

'What the hell's goin' on in there,' Seamus slurs, 'stupid louse, you're gonna wake them kids.'

He staggers towards Jason's bedroom door. He's always known it wouldn't be easy bringing up a lad like Jason, but the boy's inability, or reluctance, to talk is driving him crazy – especially after a night down the pub.

'I've give that lad a home and food to eat, 'aven't I?' he would bleat to Mary. 'What more could the blasted kid want from me? What do I really care what the loser turns out like anyways? It's not like he's me own flesh and blood. And you've never wanted 'im livin' wi' us in the first place.'

But right now his priority is keeping the noise down and that means confronting Jason.

If the twins hear that racket there'll be merry hell to pay, both of 'em are impossible to shut up once they start bleatin' in the night.

Mary's no bloody use either – sleeps through anythin' – nowt but a lazy whore, she is.

'What you got in there?' Seamus stutters, roughly pushing Jason's door open.

Jason stuffs the cassette player under his pillow.

'Come on… let's 'ave a look?'

Oh, God, no! Jason stares at Seamus in a blind panic – he's had too many again – of all the times to get plastered he's gone and done it when I've got some gear in my room. Now I'll be in for it.

'Come on then. What's that ruddy noise, where's it comin' from? You been thievin' again, you miserable waster?' Seamus pulls Jason to his feet by his sweatshirt.

The first drunken blow is aim perfect, catching Jason unawares, landing square on the bridge of his nose.

'You stupid thick-'eaded sod,' growls Seamus, shaking Jason's shoulders. 'I got a good mind to knock the livin' daylights out of you for good. If you 'ad 'alf a brain you'd be ruddy dangerous. Where's this stuff come from, eh? Where? Tell me, lad!'

A smell of stale beer wafts up Jason's bloodied nose. His fists clench and he feels the old anger rising within.

He looks into Seamus' eyes but sees Stefan staring back at him instead. Screwing his eyes up tightly, a hatred ferments from his gut up into his throat.

It's all going to go wrong if I don't put a lid on it … and soon. I have to act now before I do something and everything gets ruined.

Flicking Seamus' hand away with his arm, Jason pummels his chest earnestly with his finger, mouthing, 'mine, it's mine.'

Seamus squints at Jason through a drunken veil. 'Like hell it is,' he slurs. 'You've nicked this. You're *scum* and you'll pay. I'll make sure o' it.'

Then Seamus turns as if to leave.

Jason exhales restlessly; his breathing short and jagged; he needs to sit down all of a sudden; the room is swaying and he feels faint.

He doesn't notice Seamus swivel back around on his heels to face him once again. He only feels the crunch of someone else's fist against his left cheek.

Staggering, his hands instinctively pulled up to protect his face, Jason groans with the searing pain of dislocated bone.

Seamus straightens out his hand calmly, stretches his fingers and meanders out of the room, pulling the door closed behind him and leaving Jason to his silent agony.

He can taste it now.

Skulking in the dim light he moans, eyes closed, senses dizzy and confused as he swallows blood that trickles down over his swollen gums and between his teeth. It floods the back of his mouth and he retches, cupping his hands in front of his mouth to catch it. Staggering over to his bed, he pushes open the window and spits waves of blood and saliva down onto the silent street below.

Searching out an old cushion from the bottom of the wardrobe, Jason presses it softly against his swollen cheek for some support before lying down on his bed.

Tensing the fingers of his free hand, he stretches the sinews and tendons to form a tight, white fist. The blood surges through his veins, warming the taut hard muscle of his forearm.

Jason squeezes the plumped pillow beneath his head and imagines it is Seamus' contorted face – mimicking the noise of crunching bone as his grip tightens on the fabric, wishing his revenge could be as sweet … and as simple, as that.

I could hurt Seamus if I *really* wanted to. I really could, but there's no point. He can't damage me, not really.

He can't get right inside my mind like Stefan did.

And it reassures Jason to believe that Seamus could be at his mercy … if only in his head.

PART SIX

Life is prosperous in the back streets of a small town for a young criminal like Jason. He is fast enough to outpace the old people and quick witted enough to elude the law.

Jason's reputation grows. Together with his friend, Tom, a most willing accomplice, they make a formidable team. Tom's father owns the local newsagents and his family live above the shop. It's a shabby place, striped ripped awnings covered with mould drape over the front window, broken crates of empties are stacked precariously high by the backdoor. The shop stands set back on the pavement on a busy junction. Between the *posh* and the *poor*, Tom always says. The *poor* being where Jason lives and the *posh* being where the two boys spend their evenings raiding well stocked garages, immaculate gardens and the luxurious homes of wealthy businessmen and their families. The newsagents is their unofficial head office, with its continual supply of snacks and drinks courtesy of Tom's sleight of hand and, more importantly, at holiday-times Tom can find out who has cancelled their newspapers – sometimes for a whole week or more – giving them unrestricted access to empty properties.

'This is the life,' Tom laughs, pouring them both a coke from a giant larder fridge. 'Blimey! Look at this freezer. It's stashed with all sorts. Want an ice-lolly?'

Jason reclines on a leather settee in the huge living area, feet up on the arms, staring at a giant flat-screen television screwed to the wall.

I never believed people really lived like this, he thinks to himself. How come *they've* got all this stuff and I've got *nothing*? It's not fair.'

Tom nudges Jason, ice-lolly seeping through his fingers with a steady drip, drip, drip onto the shiny wooden floor. 'They must be loaded,' he says. 'Been upstairs yet?'

The floor in the hallway is polished wood; a long oak table extends from the bottom of the stairs to the middle of the room. It is covered with a cream cloth and on it rests a giant bowl filled with colourful stones and shells. Jason grabs a handful and heads up the stairs, juggling them badly as he goes. He stares up at a crystal chandelier hanging from a gold chain, throws a stone up at it and smiles. The stone clinks on the glass, shaking the chandelier before falling back down onto the hall floor and chipping into the beautiful stained wood.

Jason laughs and throws another. Serves them right, he thinks, shouldn't have so much money, greedy sods…

Tom then follows suit, collects a handful of stones and chases Jason up the stairs. Soon they are both hurling stones and shells at the light fitting, laughing as it sways, shards of glass splintering and clattering to the floor below, shattering on the wood like pebbles on ice. They stop only when they have run out of stones and the chandelier is nothing more than an ugly metal frame.

The sight of it pleases Jason and he sighs contentedly at the destruction he has caused.

'Do you know who lives here?' asks Tom.

Jason shakes his head.

'Well I do. I know they get *The Guardian* anyway,' Tom says knowledgeably, 'and they like cooking and they have a girl who likes horses.' Tom taps his nose. 'You should call me Sherlock, Jason, my old mate.'

Jason looks perplexed.

'They have magazines delivered from the shop, see?' continues Tom, 'they must be *billionaires* or something. A newspaper *every* day and two magazines a month! And bloody hell, Jase! Look at this…' Tom swings open a pair of gold trimmed double doors into a master bedroom the size of their school sports hall.

'Crikey, this whole carpet is like a giant bloody sheepskin rug!' squeals Tom, diving onto the king size bed. 'Fancy a ciggy? They got hundreds in a cupboard on the landing out there.'

I need a pee, thinks Jason. Bet they've got loads of bathrooms. But he can't be bothered looking… so instead, he urinates against the bedroom wall, laughing as it drips down the flock wallpaper onto the expensive fibres of the cream carpet beneath.

'Come on,' says Tom at last, 'let's get what we can and get out of here.'

By the middle of October, Jason and Tom have amassed a considerable stash of valuables from their evening raids. They hide everything in one of the old garages at the back of Railway Street.

Nobody would think to look there. Most of the garages are derelict buildings with warped and rusted up and over doors.

The garage at the far end is boarded up. Its green metal door is barely visible behind the batons of flaking wood roughly nailed to the frontage, along with a mass of choking ivy. This is the one they choose.

There are two panels along one side that have been loose for some time and when Tom and Jason pull them away they discover a perfect storehouse for their stolen treasure. Everything will be safe here until they find buyers for their goods, for nobody in their rightful mind *ever* walks down the alley behind Railway Street at night. The houses there are small and square with regimented little gardens tended lovingly each afternoon by old men in brown trousers and white shirts. By nightfall their gardens have been fed and watered and their curtains closed on the outside world. Jason and Tom often walk the full length of the street before turning up the alley to their garage – always after dark – always making sure nobody is watching.

They have been frequenting the garage at the back of Railway Street for some months, when one evening they notice a shadowy outline in the front window of number eleven.

They ignore it at first.

Whoever it is won't be able to see much from there, so they think nothing more of the matter and saunter arrogantly by as usual, turning up the alley towards the garage with their stolen loot.

As the weeks go by the person in the shadows starts to unnerve them.

They don't like being spied on, it could ruin everything. But still the ghostly form stands and watches, steadfast and unwavering.

The two boys start to stare back as they pass, glowering at the shape in the darkness, clenching their fists and hoping whoever it is might take the hint and leave them alone. But the haunting figure seems fixed, resolute in its contemplation of them.

It is Halloween when Jason's curiosity finally gets the better of him.

He ventures to number eleven Railway Street without Tom, leaving Mary in the kitchen at home ironing and Seamus presumably in the pub.

On the way he passes scruffy kids dressed as stripy winceyette ghosts and cackling bin-bag witches and strange cardboard pumpkins painted bright orange.

'Woo! Woo!' shouts one little boy from beneath a blanket. Jason delves into his pocket but can only find a half-opened packet of chewing gum.

Scary ghost, he thinks, smiling, giving him the gum.

The boy runs off into the shadows.

It is only about six-thirty in the evening, but it is dark outside and an eerie chill wraps itself around Jason's chest as he reaches number eleven. Forcing a deep breath, he looks through the front room window.

The room is empty. But the front door is ajar and Jason's hand trembles as he grasps the polished handle.

Perhaps they're expecting someone, he wonders, for who leaves their front door open after dark at Halloween?

Jason walks into the hallway.

He can smell old people and damp and furniture polish. The hallway is dimly lit. A walking stick and old-fashioned hat hang on a coat rack at the bottom of the stairs. Walking on tiptoes, Jason is careful not to make any sound at all. One false move from you, whoever you are, and you'll be sorry, he thinks, imagining the look on someone's face when he bursts through the door.

'Hello? Who's there?' A clipped voice resonates from somewhere deep in the back of the house.

Excellent, decides Jason, an *old* man! Won't have much trouble with you...

There is a noise from a radio or TV and Jason whistles expectantly. There are always people happy to buy second-hand sets these days.

He is glad he has come tonight. It won't be a wasted journey.

'Is that you, Mrs O'Leary?' says the clipped voice. 'I don't need any help this evening, thank you. I've managed to peel my own potatoes and I've put a lamb chop in the oven for my supper.'

Jason puts his hand over his mouth to prevent a snigger escaping. Who the hell is Mrs O'Leary? This old chap's going to have a coronary when he sees me. And on reaching the room where the noise is coming from, Jason thrusts the door open.

But once inside, he sucks in a deep breath. His body is encased by a sudden chill, rigid with unexpected fear and confusion.

Two steely grey eyes fix on him from the other side of the room. A tall man with pallid features stands up from his chair by the fireside.

'So it's you?' the tall man says, calmly.

Jason frowns and circles anxiously around the room, his hands by his sides.

'I'm glad you've come,' the man adds.

Jason stares down at the lino. He can smell meat cooking and the room is stifling with the heat coming from the oven.

Something in his head tells him to run away. You're in *danger,* you are out of your depth it screams, silently.

And yet he *can't* leave – Jason can't turn and go now he's finally arrived, he can't avoid facing up to whatever it is that has brought him here … not yet. Instead he licks his lips and tries hard to stem the thudding in his chest.

I know you, he thinks despondently, staring at the man warily, from under his fringe. I know you but I don't think we've ever met before today.

Jason presses his fingers to his forehead, runs his hands roughly across his scalp to ease his tremor, to soothe his restless soul and resolve the absurd notions that are running riot in his head.

'Why have you come to me?' the old man asks.

Jason's tongue is numb, his throat thick and heavy and it is hard to swallow.

The clammy heat makes Jason's hair stick to the back of his neck.

'I … I've come because you told me to,' Jason stutters at last, shocked by his clumsy garble.

It is his own voice; and these are the first words he has spoken out loud to anybody – let alone a complete stranger – for well over four years. Their strange resonance echoes in the room long after their meaning fades away.

And Jason hopes he sounds normal, for whilst he has spoken quietly to himself often in the privacy of his room, he cannot be sure of the accuracy of speech after being silent for so very long.

The old man smiles. 'I *didn't* tell you to, sonny,' he says softly, 'but I knew you *would* come. You had to one day. And I'm glad of that…'

'I can't stay long, I've got to go soon … now, actually,' Jason stammers, every thread of instinct screaming at him to turn and flee. 'My friends are outside,' he lies, 'they'll be wondering where I am.'

It is a whole week and three days before Jason plucks up the courage to return to number eleven Railway Street. He really should forget about the dingy house and the old man with the steely eyes who seems to see right inside his soul.

But he can't.

There is nobody by the window the second time, but all the same his spine stiffens involuntarily as he pushes open the gate and walks up the path to the front door.

Through the window Jason can see the shadowy outline of furniture, soft shapes illuminated by shafts of light streaming through the door into the hallway.

But where is the old man?

Is he expecting Jason?

Perhaps he is waiting in the kitchen like last time?

Jason taps on the door, lightly at first for he isn't really sure he wants to be heard. The door swings open immediately.

'Come in,' says the old man pleasantly, standing in the hallway, before turning and walking away towards the kitchen. Once inside, he bends down to warm his hands in front of a roaring log stove, waiting for Jason to follow him in.

'Close the door if you will, sonny. Keep the heat in.'

Jason does as he is told. Then there is a silence. Jason shuffles anxiously, unsure of what he should do next.

'Why, I've quite forgotten my manners,' the old man offers, eventually. 'Arnold Greenhalgh,' and he stretches a hand out towards Jason. 'I'm *very* pleased to meet you at long last.'

Nobody has ever offered to shake Jason's hand before. He takes a nifty step backwards. 'Jason,' he says awkwardly, 'I ... I shouldn't have come back. I'll be going now, shall I?'

Jason's gaze darts to the door – senses alert, twitching – he's ready to flee if he needs to.

Arnold smiles, his hand still stretched out invitingly, moving nearer to Jason, fixing him with a firm, unavoidable stare.

'Please yourself, sonny,' he says slowly, nodding, 'but I've been watching you for some time now. You and that friend of yours, trespassing ... thieving ... stalking old people like me.'

Jason is at the door now, cornered, grasping the handle shakily. So that's what it's all about, he thinks, breathlessly, his whole body on fire, ready to run yet willing to explode right here and now if this old man carries on much longer.

You don't frighten me, he thinks. I could sort you out right now if I really wanted to, but I'm going now and *you* can't stop me.

'There's no need to leave so soon,' says the old man lightly, as though he can read Jason's mind and as though he already regrets what he has just said. His voice is softer now, soothing...

'Actually I could use a little help around the place – I could give you a few odd jobs to do. Would you like that? I would pay you, of course – I struggle to cope on my own these days... since... since I lost my dear wife.' At the mention of his wife, the old man's voice cracks and he moves even nearer to Jason, too close, fixing him with those grey steely eyes that stare right into his soul.

Jason can't take any more.

He lurches towards the door handle. 'I've ... I've got to go,' he stammers, turning the handle frantically both ways. 'But I'll come again,' he adds, out of the blue, 'I will. I promise.'

PART SEVEN

Three days later Jason finds himself on Railway Street again.

For a moment he stands at the end of Arnold's path, gazing up at the bay window, wondering if he should go in.

Arnold is in his usual place.

On seeing Jason, he draws closer to the glass and waves. Jason pushes open the gate and, without a second thought, walks up the path.

Soon he is standing in the tiny, cluttered dining room. It smells damp and musty, as though it hasn't been heated properly for a while.

'I rarely use this room these days,' Arnold explains. 'Doesn't seem any point now I'm on my own.'

In one corner is an upright piano, faded and dusty, these days – nothing more than a shelf for photographs and memories. Jason wanders over and picks up a picture of a man in uniform. He has grey eyes and a dark moustache. The colour is faded, the photo ragged around the edges, but Jason recognises those eyes immediately.

'You?'

Arnold nods. 'France, 1940 – I was there until the evacuation.'

Jason puts the photo down.

This old man can keep his sorry tale. I'm not hanging around here to listen to stories.

'Why exactly are you here again, young man?' asks Arnold gently, as if delving into Jason's thoughts.

Jason shrugs his shoulders, for he's not quite sure himself yet and he reaches out to pick up another picture. There are lots of men in this one – all of them smiling, shirtsleeves rolled up – arms clasped around each other's shoulders.

The old man takes the photo from him gently. 'I look at this one more than the others. There's only two of us left now,' he says, pointing a lean finger in turn at two of the men on the back row. He shakes his head as if he can't quite believe the others have gone, drawing the photo up to his face to get a closer look.

The photo shivers in the old man's tired, gnarled hands.

'They were good times, sonny. We were only kids, you know, but we all stuck together. Where's that Dunkirk spirit now, eh?' And he looks at Jason expectantly.

Jason peers down at the floor. 'Dunno. Don't know what you're talking about.'

'I'm talking about *war,* sonny, *war!*' The man's eyes spark, ignite, suddenly alive with passion.

'*That's* what I mean,' he says, picking up a newspaper from the chair behind him and pointing to the adverts. 'We don't know we're born these days ... sliced bread, microwave meals, Boeing 747 to take us on our holidays, blasted computers to do all our work for us. I'll tell you what I'm talking about, sonny ...' and he claps his hands together, scattering the pages of the newspaper over the floor. 'It was *war* that made us great. And I'm not just talking about the fighting either – I mean the unity – the spirit. Everyone working together, caring, prepared to sacrifice their lives for others ... you don't come home and just forget it all like *that.*' He clicks his fingers. 'It stays with you, makes you who you are, moulds you, carves you for the rest of your life.'

Jason jumps. He wonders whether or not he should gather the pages of newspaper up, but Arnold gives him a warning glance as if to say stay where you are, fixing Jason rigidly to the spot. You're mad, decides Jason warily, not daring to move and saying the first thing that comes into his head, anything to break the silence that has descended over them.

'I think war sounds good. There are a few people I'd like to beat up good and proper, people who don't like me, always want to hurt me.' And he thinks of the boys in the playground, and of what he'd like to do to Stefan, even after all this time.

'I'm good at fighting – always been a fighter – always needed to be, see? Fighting's what makes me tick. It's like ... like my *thing*.'

Arnold's eyes darken. 'Your *thing*?' he spits, face dark and penetrating. 'Let me tell you something, sonny ... I don't believe kids like you will *ever* know what we went through back then and I hope for your sake that's always the case. War is nobody's *thing*.'

Then he looks away, vaguely. 'But I suppose you cannot possibly be expected to understand just yet ... you will though, you will, sonny ... when the time comes.'

'Understand what?'

'That you're going about it the wrong way, that you are *misguided*. War is not an excuse for hatred and intolerance and jealousy and all those emotions that you seem to be so proud of exhibiting to the world. I've seen you, sonny, I've seen you strutting up and down the street with your friend. I've seen you breaking into houses, stealing from vulnerable old people who have done nothing to you, who don't deserve to be victimised and bullied; for that's what you are – nothing but a bully – and what *you* take part in is violent, mindless aggression ... just short of murder really ... but definitely *not* real war. You bear no resemblance to the men on these photos. Don't ever mistake the two, sonny. War has a purpose, war is about love, what *you* do is merely an excuse for hatred.

War is about doing all you can to defend what's important – it's about striving for understanding and peace.'

Jason flinches. Miss Lemon and the others always called him violent and Mary still often refers to him as *that murderin' thug*. How come this old guy knows so much, anyway?

'So is that *all* you fought for … love and unity and peace?' Jason cannot hide the disappointment in his voice.

Arnold slams his hand down on the top of the piano, the photos scatter noisily and Jason jumps again. 'There is nothing else worth fighting for. You will find that out one day. One day, when the time comes, you will realise that the only thing really worth fighting for is love.'

Jason stifles a yawn.

He's fed up.

The old man is talking rubbish.

'I can't stay much longer,' he lies, 'the others will be wondering where I am. Last time I came you said there might be some jobs for me to do. I need the money, see?'

'Ah, yes,' Arnold rummages through an overflowing letter rack on the mantelpiece.

'Here it is – my list – just let me get my glasses and I'll be with you in a jiffy.' He breezes out of the room, returning a moment or two later with reading glasses perched on the end of his nose, reeling off a list that has been scrawled on the back of an old cereal packet.

'Fuse box – wiring needs looking at – seem to have some sort of problem with the bathroom light. I could do it myself of course, but the fingers aren't up to much these days.' He holds up his hands to reveal his knuckles – worn, split twigs of gnarled flesh.

'And there's a problem with a hinge on one of the kitchen cupboards. Keeps coming off. Probably just needs longer screws. It's a real nuisance getting old, Jason, it really is. Your body lets you down more and more with each passing day. Now come on, roll your sleeves up, sonny, and let's get cracking.'

And, before Jason can think any more about making a run for it, Arnold leads him to a dark pantry where he shines a strong beam on rows of fuse-boxes before handing Jason a screwdriver and inviting him to step inside.

'I'll tell you which colour wire needs to be in which socket. You just make sure it's right or we could both end up in outer space.'

Jason scratches his head. 'This is mad. I'm colour blind, you know?'

'No need to worry, sonny, I'll talk you through it. Trust me and we'll work just fine as a team.'

Barely fifteen minutes later, Jason hands the screwdriver back to the old man, wipes his hands together with a sublime and strange sense of satisfaction and follows Arnold to the bathroom door.

Arnold takes a deep breath, pulls the cord and illuminates the room in glorious light.

'Marvellous! Well done, sonny! It's not been easy taking a bath in the dark! Come on, it's late. I'll show you to the door.'

They make their way along the hallway.

'What's that on your arm?' Jason asks, as Arnold starts to unroll the sleeves of his brown sweater.

'A sailing boat – had it done in France, we all had one – this bit was added later,' he says, pulling his sleeve up again to show Jason two names and the number six hundred and ninety-three in black italics.

Jason moves closer to get a better look. 'Who's *Jane*? Hey, you've got *two* girls names there. That's dangerous, isn't it?'

Arnold strokes the tattoo protectively. 'Those two girls saved my life, sonny. But there were many more I can tell you … many, *many* more.'

When they reach the front door the old man opens it and moves aside to let Jason leave.

'Why *did* you join up in the first place if you don't like war?' Jason asks, stopping in the doorway.

'No choice, I was called to serve King and Country. But it was the best – and worst – thing that ever happened to me.'

'How do you mean?'

'It made me sharper, cleverer. It took me away from my family but it also removed me from the confines of my everyday life; it made me sit up and take notice of the world and it made me understand what really matters. I learnt lots of things during wartime – skills, disciplines, knowledge that I never knew were important before … just like wiring, I suppose … and in wartime those things can make the difference between life and death.'

'I don't get you.'

Arnold holds out his arm as though he can see something in the distance skulking up the garden path. Jason looks out into the dark street too, but he can only see night-time and a cat ambling along the garden wall.

The old man starts to whisper in short jagged breaths. 'The enemy is attacking from the West. There are many more of them than there are of you and you must attack them when they are at their most vulnerable to stand any chance of survival. There are two points of access for them. One is through a valley between two ridges in the East and the other is across the river. The choice is yours. Where would you send your men in an attempt to divert the enemy?'

'Don't know,' stutters Jason blankly, desperate to say the right thing but only able to feebly shrug his shoulders in defeat.

'Well, there you go then,' Arnold hisses loudly, slouching on one leg and folding his arms as if to prove his point. 'You'd be dead and so would all your men. If you send your men to the wrong place you're in trouble, big trouble.' He leans his head down towards Jason and nods omnisciently. 'But if you had done your homework, if you had prior knowledge, then you would know the valley is barely accessible even on foot and, as the enemy will be weighed down by heavy artillery, they would be quite unable to cut through that way. So you get your men to plant civilian boats upstream on the opposite shore in the hope the enemy will try and use them to cross the river. You've got them, sonny. You send all your men to the riverside and wait for them to arrive.'

'That's not fighting, that's brain surgery,' says Jason.

'War isn't for morons, sonny. You have to be quick-witted, on your toes, ready for anything.'

'Are you having a go? I'm no moron. Are you calling me an idiot?' Jason rises to his full height, suddenly snatching a glimpse of the old man's wallet on the telephone shelf behind him in the hallway. He may as well make use of the visit. The old man won't put up too much of a fight. He's way past his best.

'You're a loser. Just like the others ...' Jason mutters tensely, shifting his weight nervously from one foot to the other, staring hard at the wallet, 'you all think I'm no good but you're *all* wrong. It's easy for you. I bet you were clever to start with. I bet you had a mum and a dad and a nice home and all that?'

Arnold traps Jason's wandering eyes, studding his steely gaze between Jason and the wallet on the table. 'Maybe I *am* a loser as you so bluntly put it. I'm certainly no genius. And I am beginning to think maybe I am very, *very* wrong about you after all...'

'Huh?'

'I certainly couldn't mend a fuse-box at your age,' he continues 'but I knew enough not to get into trouble with the law – and it's got nothing to do with having a nice home or not. You can't go through life blaming everyone else, sonny. Sometimes you have to look inside yourself to make change happen. Here …' and he picks up the wallet that Jason has been staring at for so long. Taking out a crisp twenty-pound note, he presses it into Jason's hand.

'Take it. Theft never pays. An honest job is worth its weight in gold – this is for helping me today. I appreciate it very much. Thank you, Jason.'

Jason has never seen a twenty-pound note before. He slides it into his pocket, keeps a soft hold on it to make sure he doesn't lose it, stroking the smooth crisp edges, struggling to look Arnold in the eyes.

'You'll come good eventually,' soothes Arnold, staring hard at Jason, holding out his hand to the young man. 'You've got a choice. I know you'll do the right thing when the time comes.'

'If there's anything else you need doing … I'll … I'll do it next time, shall I?' says Jason, feeling the firm undeniable clasp of Arnold's hand in his.

And, as Jason walks down the path, he turns back and they smile at one another, boy to man, friend to friend. For they both know there will be a next time.

PART EIGHT

By the time Jason is fourteen, Seamus practically lives in the
pub and Mary has given up on trying to keep either of them
on the straight and narrow. It's hard enough forcing the twins
into submission every day and Seamus is never there to help,
so why should Mary even be bothered with the *murderin'*
thug?

Jason, in turn, has nothing to do with his guardians.

It is a mutually acceptable arrangement.

He cares nothing for their lives and they his.

His apathy has become so all consuming that he even
speaks to them occasionally these days. There is little point
keeping up the silence anymore. It seemed such a good idea
to keep his mouth shut all those years ago – when they
shouted at him and constantly nagged him to tell them what
really happened *that* night at The Home. And besides, it all
seems so different now he has met Arnold. All the anxiety
and fear subsides when he is with the old man. He doesn't
worry so much about the future and about what it does or
doesn't hold or can or cannot provide.

It is as though Jason steps outside the narrow boundaries
of his own body and mind when he is in the company of
Arnold and, in so doing, absorbs some of the old man's
infinite wisdom.

'Why borrow tomorrow's worries and concerns, sonny,
for we all know tomorrow never really comes?' Arnold
always says. 'The past has gone. It has a habit of doing that
you know – you just have to move on and do your best
today.'

And that is what Jason wants to do.

But all the same, Seamus' face was an absolute picture the first time he heard Jason speak.

'I'm going out tonight,' Jason announced coolly, one evening, as Seamus arrived home from work, '...and I'll be back late.'

Seamus turned and stared at him for a second or two. 'What did you say, boy?'

Jason repeated it again.

'Mary, Mary, here, quick!'

Seamus grabbed Mary and thrust her in front of Jason.

'Tell her, boy.'

'I said I am going out and I'll probably be back very late. If you've got a problem with that you can kiss my ...'

'Holy Mother of God be praised!' Mary fell to the floor, 'that school has worked miracles.'

Jason stepped over her slumped body and walked silently out of the house. It's got nothing to do with miracles, he thought, as the evening sun warmed his face. It's about choice, and it's about Arnold. I've *chosen* to speak and that's the end of it.

But all the same, he felt a powerful sense of satisfaction as he walked away down the street, his eyes focussed firmly on the road ahead.

It's now three years since Jason first met Arnold.

He still hasn't told the others about him.

They would surely laugh at the thought of Jason befriending a weak old man and would no doubt do their level best to persuade him to steal from him. He couldn't bring himself to even think about it – not after all this time – but goodness knows it wouldn't be difficult.

'I can't go on the make tonight,' he whispers on the telephone to Tom when Mary is out of earshot, '... grounded again.'

Tom sighs loudly, 'what you done *this* time? Caught again? You really got to stop being so careless, Jase. I need you – thieving needs two – I can't do it the same on my own.'

'I know, sorry mate, I'll make it soon, I will,' a superficial whine of remorse floating down the wire as Jason tries to sound downcast.

Then he hangs up sharply and rushes out of the house in the direction of Arnold's.

Approaching the junction at the end of Furnace Street, he has a quick look to make sure nobody is watching before taking the familiar sharp left into Railway Street. He doesn't like all this furtive nonsense. He feels like a spy. All the cloak and dagger stuff grinds him down, but the consequences of Tom finding out about Arnold are just too unbearable to consider. He would either want to steal from him or, even worse, Arnold would become Tom's friend too.

And Jason isn't ready to share the old man with anyone just yet…

It is seven-thirty.

Arriving at number eleven, Jason pushes open the wooden gate as usual and looks to see if the old man is in his usual spot by the window.

He is.

Arnold beckons Jason inside and invites him to sit down.

They are easily on first name terms these days. Jason has never called an adult by their christian name before but Arnold insists. 'We're friends,' he says, 'and friends mustn't stand on ceremony with one another.'

Arnold pours a cup of tea. His wrist shakes as he passes the teacup to Jason. The teacup wobbles right off the saucer, hot liquid sloshing to the floor, scalding the old man on the arm as it gushes in streams onto the carpet beneath.

Jason jumps up and sucks in a sharp breath. 'Sorry, sorry! Oh God, sorry! I'll go get a cloth. I will. I'll go now.' And he sprints to the kitchen, flustered, heart beating recklessly, eyes darting across the worktops for something to mop up the spillage.

On returning to the sitting room, he finds Arnold sipping tea in a state of calm sobriety, as though nothing has happened.

'I'm fine young Jason, just a slight scald, nothing to worry about, really. But thank you for your obvious concern.'

Jason squeezes the damp cloth between his shaking fingers. He takes another strained breath and steadies his strangely racing heart.

There are no harsh words or punishment – there are only remnants of childlike fear instilled in him by The Home that still lodge deep in his soul.

He imagines Miss Lemon, Stefan's haunting face, the nights in the cellar, thrashings across his back from the leather belt, the pain and hunger.

But it is different now, it really is. Yet he still cannot truly understand this peace that hangs so silently between him and the old man.

He stares at Arnold and wonders if he dares assume it will always feel like this.

And far above the spirits smile as they look down and nod their heads, for they know Jason has no need to be afraid … and when the time comes, so will he.

'Are you happy with your lot, sonny?' Arnold asks him later that evening. 'Do you feel your life is all it should be?'

Jason hunches his shoulders and frowns. 'Dunno.'

'Oh, come, come. Do you feel pleased with all you have achieved? Do you smile when you wake up in the morning? Is life wonderful?'

Jason shakes his head.

'Why not?'

'Nobody really likes me except you. The kids at school think I'm a loser; even Tom, who's supposed to be my mate, he only hangs around with me because we ... we ... oh, it doesn't matter why. Seamus and Mary wish I were dead. Everyone back at The Home hated me, kept me on the outside, made me different. I didn't belong there. I guess I still don't belong anywhere... won't ever ... not really.'

There is a tremor in Jason's voice. 'But I just ... I just wanted them to be my friends ... it sounds corny, you know, but I wanted them to like me just a little bit ... it never happened ... and now it's too late.'

Arnold scratches his forehead. 'They don't sound like nice folk to me. But you must have done *something* to make them like that, surely?'

'What are you, some sort of shrink?'

Arnold holds his hands up. 'No, I'm just a silly retired bus-driver who wants to help, that's all. Sometimes you seem so distant and frightened, as if you're not sure how I'm going to react, as if you think I might lash out or hit you. I'm your friend, sonny, someone who has your best interests at heart. Believe me, please. But tell me to mind my own business if you really don't want to talk about it. I will quite understand ... we all have things we'd rather forget ...'

Jason swallows hard. 'There's nothing to tell. When I left The Home they all said I was bad. I used to get angry – really mad – fighting and everything, but *they* made me like that. *They* knew what to do and *they* all thought it was funny. And then I ... then I hurt someone and I had to leave.'

'But you must have been glad to be going. You didn't like it there one bit from what you've said, did you?'

There is a silence. 'Yes, no, well it's complicated. I didn't want to leave in a way because ...'

'Yes? Go on, sonny ...'

'Because of my sea.' Jason's face burns red, but a fiery spark in his eyes and the excitement in his voice contradict his blushes.

'The Home is next to the dunes, by the sea ... my sea – somewhere – miles away from here. I don't know where. But I do know nobody else cared about it, neither the ocean nor the beach, the sky nor the wind and storms.

Nobody saw it like I did.

I loved it all.

And all those boats – like coloured fish racing across the bay – you wouldn't believe it even if you saw them.

I still see them now – dream about them – they're in here,' and Jason taps his head. 'Am I mad or what?'

He feels ridiculous, a small awkward child again. 'I've never told anybody before...'

'Those are fine things to think about,' Arnold cuts in. 'You carry on dreaming of those boats, sonny, for my guess is that you miss them terribly and you need them like crazy?'

Jason blows out a mouthful of air and sighs. Why does Arnold have to be right all the time?

It hasn't hurt quite so much until now.

A deep knot rankles and grinds from inside. He sinks his fingernails into his palms like he used to do and tries to steady his breathing.

'Why should I bother? What does any of it matter anyway? I will always be a failure,' he whispers, 'my boats aren't even real – but they're all I've got.'

'No, Jason, you are quite wrong. Your boats *are* real. And how on earth can you consider yourself to be a failure?

Men died so the likes of you and I could live the lives of our choosing. We have a duty to make their sacrifice worthwhile, to make something of ourselves.'

Then the old man goes to a bureau in a corner of the sitting room and pulls out a cardboard file held together with elastic bands.

He beckons Jason to the settee and sits down next to him, letting the contents of the file – newspaper cuttings, letters and photographs – all spill across his lap. Then he picks up the first scrap of newsprint and reads out the headline, *the miracle of Dunkirk.*

'Haven't looked at these in years,' he says, sadly.

'What's a miracle?' asks Jason.

'If you'd not bunked off school so much you'd already know.'

'But ...'

'... It's something wonderful that you can't quite explain ... or perhaps believe at the time it's happening, something you would consider impossible but it really, really does happen. See this man here?' And Arnold flicks through the first few photos on the pile before pulling one out to show Jason. He points to a pale man in an army uniform on the back row. 'That's George Fogg. I first met him when I was nine and on holiday with my parents in Bournemouth.

It was a grand holiday.

Dad bought me a sailing ship.

My, it was a beauty. You could adjust the sail and the rudder and it had a sturdy rope to pull it along with. Toys like that don't matter these days but it was precious then, money was scarce and a gift from my father, special.

I remember playing with it in the sea every day. I got drenched, rolled my trousers up as high as they would go but they still got wet – always went in too deep, you see.

Then one day, somehow my boat got snagged, the tide was coming in fast and I remember my Dad shouting frantically from the shore telling me to let it go and to come out of the water. There was this fishing boat passing not far away, it had its name painted on the side in curvy black letters – *Thelmar* – I remember it to this day, a pretty ship, glossy and sleek. And as it glided by I could see my little boat near it, bobbing up and down frantically, little sail flapping as it tried to stay afloat in the undercurrent.

I cried and shouted to the man in the boat, asking him to save it and pull it from the dirty sea, but he didn't.

He was a nice enough young chap though, and I think he felt guilty that he hadn't been able to reach down and save my lovely little boat. He let me sit in *Thelmar* later that afternoon when he'd pulled her onto the sand. I'd never been as close as that to a real boat before. It was exciting, but it didn't make up for losing my toy one.

George and I became pen friends after that holiday. He was fifteen but he seemed a lot younger – a bit like you really. He'd bunked off once too often – wasn't the greatest writer, to tell you the truth, not the best pen friend to be sure. His letters were always short and badly spelt. All George wanted was to become a real fisherman like his father. We lost touch when war broke out.'

'But you met up again,' announces Jason, 'or he wouldn't be in that photo with you?'

Arnold nods, 'quite right sonny, quite right. All these men here were like brothers to me.'

'So … what about the miracle?'

'It happened on a beach in France.

We were inland and we received orders to head for the coast. The Germans were advancing and we had little defence against their artillery.

It took us days and days to get to the beach, marching solidly around the clock – sometimes up to forty miles a day – our feet were ripped to bits, no skin left, just sores and the like. And we had no food either, just water we found in streams and puddles, leaves, maggots, anything to give us enough energy to carry on walking.

The people in the villages were kind enough. They threw food at us if they could, left bags on street corners with dry bread and meat fat in.

And all the while, bombs fell on either side of us – innocent people killed – sights you don't want to think about but that stay lodged in your mind forever. You can't shake them away, see. There were people crying to us for help, arms outstretched, bloodied, dying.'

Arnold bows his head, his voice barely audible. 'We left so many wounded along the way. Couldn't risk slowing down. If we'd waited for the stragglers, we'd all have been gunned down or bombed – lost the best friends I ever had on that dusty, dirty roadside – can still see their faces clearly to this day if I close my eyes and ...' Arnold grips the newspaper cutting tightly to his chest, offering a silent prayer to the heavens '... and I'll never forgive myself for that, sonny. Not ever.'

Tears well up behind the old man's glasses. 'When we finally arrived at the beach, all the British army vehicles had been assembled in advance. Our first job was to blow them up.'

'Blow them up? You're kidding? Great! But why?'

'Well, we couldn't leave them behind for the Germans to use.'

'Then what?'

'We stayed where we were for the next four days. There were thousands of us. Can you imagine that many of us,

Jason, all afraid, all uncertain if we were going to live or die? Nobody had a clue what was going on.

Retreat was our only option, but when we ran out of land and all that was left was the sea, we were scared I can tell you; more scared than you could ever imagine.

Boys not much older than you lay covered in blood with arms or legs missing, others blinded by shells, screaming and crying for their mothers.

It was the worst sight on earth.

That is the futility of war, Jason, the harsh truth of combat. It's not pretty or glamorous.

The bombs just kept falling everywhere.

Nobody was safe.

And planes were circling overhead all day and all night, clouding the skies with their enormous steel wings and droning engines that never let up. The noise Jason, the noise …'

Arnold covers his ears.

'You okay?' Jason strains to see the old man's face, gingerly placing a hand on his shoulder. Arnold nods.

'I was luckier than many. I had a bag of grenades and a rifle, so at least I had something to protect myself with. We could see them in the distance, coming at us over land, but we had nowhere to go. Behind us was the Channel – and England – but we would never have survived in those waters.'

'Why didn't you fight them with your guns and grenades?'

'We did – when we had to – but the enemy was bigger than us and they were much better equipped than we were.'

'The enemy?' Jason begins, 'the Germans?'

'That's right. The Blitzkrieg was advancing.'

'Blitzkrieg?'

'It means *lightning war*. Their tactics were speed and surprise. They wanted to get it all over with as quickly as possible so they sent tanks, aeroplanes and many, many men to get the job done. They knew we were stranded, you see.

All we could do was hide in the sand dunes and pray.

It was all we had left. We weren't properly trained. We all had rifles, but *they* had the most up to date equipment imaginable and we stood no chance … no chance at all.

There were bodies everywhere. Dads, brothers, uncles, cousins …we were prisoners with no escape route; no food, no fresh water … just a heady stench of decay and an endless channel of murky salt water.'

'Okay, okay, I get it,' says Jason, grimacing. 'What happened after that?'

'Eric Studley, that's him on the left,' Arnold says, pointing to a wiry young man on the photograph, with wavy hair and a wide smile. 'We sneaked out together over the back of the dunes one evening to a ramshackle garage we'd noticed earlier in the day. When we got there we found it was crammed with whisky and tins of carnation milk.'

Jason screws his face up '*nasty.*'

'You'd think so, but the feast we had from that garage was better than anything I'd tasted before or since. And better still …' there is an unmistakeable twinkle now in the old man's eyes, 'we were brave that night. We were warm and fiery and full of whisky and we could have beaten the whole blasted German Army if we'd been given the chance.'

'So how *did* you get off the beach?'

'The next morning the sun was burning hot and we'd just about decided it was the end of the road for all of us. Then over the horizon … a *miracle,* sonny, nothing short of a miracle … a row of ships, just a dozen or so to start with and then the numbers swelled, filling the sea with colour and by God, with hope. All shapes and sizes, sailing across the cold grey waves towards our shore, through the bombs and the dust and the firing.'

Jason gasps, jumps to his feet and sends the cuttings and photos cascading to the floor.

'My boats! They're my boats. I can see them, Arnold, I really can, they must be mine ...'

'Well, I'm not sure whose boats they were, but they were the most welcome sight we had ever seen. Men were dragged aboard, crammed like sardines where they could fit, hanging on for their lives, the boats rolling with their loads, making their way slowly back out to sea.

Some of them headed for the bigger ships that couldn't come into the shallow waters and they left the men on board those before coming back to shore to collect more soldiers.

Others continued across the Channel to England. The bombs were still dropping, shells screeching over their heads, but they didn't care, they were going home. Hundreds came to help us that day, men risking their lives to save complete strangers. There were even some in canoes, boats dragged down with the weight, determined to keep going until they reached safety.'

'And is that the miracle?'

'Yes, mainly, but I had my own tiny miracle, you see. Eric and I were part of the rearguard for a while; our job was to hold back the German forces until most of the men had been rescued.

Eventually we were relieved by French troops who stayed on the line and allowed us to escape.

Whilst we were waiting on the beach, we started an old lorry that looked as though it had been abandoned behind the dunes. For some reason it hadn't been blown up like the others.

Lots of boats on the shore were so full of men they were completely grounded and couldn't get into the water, so we took off our trousers and tied them together to make a long length. Eric tied one end to the rear axle and I tied the other end to the boats one by one and pulled them into the water with the lorry. We must have set a dozen or so boats on their way like that.

Then we began dragging the injured to the shore, hundreds of men and boys, sonny – all afraid for their lives – we were their final hope, you see.

There was one lad in particular – his courage will stay with me forever. He was a good soul to be sure. He was injured, had blood on his shoulder – stab wound maybe – yet he was carrying the body of a young German soldier towards the shore. That moment changed me forever. It changed him too. I could see it in his eyes. That lad was affected by war more than you could ever imagine, sonny.'

Jason frowns and pulls a face. 'But why would he do that?'

'Carry the enemy to a final place of rest, honour the dead, risk his own life for the stranger who had previously tried to kill him? Because that's love, that's real love worth dying for … if you're brave enough. That boy deserved a medal if you ask me.'

'What happened to him?'

'I don't know, sonny. I helped him for a while, carried the German myself to give the poor lad a rest, left them both by a jetty wall waiting for the next boat. Did all I could.

Eventually Eric and I were called to board a small ferry that had been sent from the North of England. We ran like blazes down that beach to the ship.

It was called *Jane* something, I can't remember properly, but a shell landed too close to us as we were leaving the harbour and we capsized.

The sea was icily chilly. You can't begin to imagine how cold it was. It was June, but by Lord we were freezing.

We held onto driftwood and to each other and to anything else that was floating in the water. Eric and I sang songs together to keep our heads above water.'

'Did you get the boat upright again?'

'We held on to the hull for hours, linking arms, singing every song we could remember, keeping each other awake deep into the night, but there was no chance of that boat sailing again.

We drifted far from the shore. It was so black out there, we were just about done in, I can tell you, and we were only wearing shorts because we'd left our trousers attached to the truck. My legs and feet hurt like hell. One minute they were burning, next minute cold, numb and so very sore.

Time went on and on, hours passed and everything became quiet. We were drowsy with the cold and the rhythmic lullaby of the waves. Whenever I was on the verge of going to sleep, Eric would whisper, *there's a boat, there's a boat* and I would wake up straight away thinking our rescuers had come and we would soon be warm and safe.'

'That's cruel.'

'But that's the sort of miracle. A boat *did* arrive, out of the blue, or rather out of the black. And then I felt an arm grab mine and heave me on board.

When I saw the face of my rescuer I cried, Jason … I cried great big tears of joy – for it was George Fogg in his old fishing boat, you remember me telling you – *Thelmar* – from that holiday in Bournemouth many years earlier?

He had sailed across the Channel to help rescue the stranded soldiers – I've forgotten which regiment he belonged to – in fact I hadn't seen him face to face since I was nine.

We'd written to each other fairly frequently for a while, but then his letters fizzled out. He never was so very good at writing, spent too much time in his boat. But I recognised him straight away that night, and he me.

George Fogg saved my life.

Where he appeared from I shall never know.

It was as though he had been sent especially for me.

I believe in that sort of thing now.

I really do, Jason.

Eric always said you got what you deserved and afterwards we wondered if helping to drag the boats down to the shore earned us some sort of special dispensation for our own survival. Whatever the reason, I remember lying in the boat and somebody covering me with ripped sailcloth to keep me warm and I looked up at the sky and watched the racing clouds and circling gulls, and thanked God or whoever was out there for the miracle of life. Do you know, I even forgave George for letting my little sailing boat perish all those years ago ... and I told him so!'

Arnold smiles, but Jason manages only a dismal frown.

'It all sounds kind of *religious*, like someone was watching out for you. And how come people risked their lives to cross the Channel to save total strangers? That's stupid.'

'People didn't think like that in those days, sonny. Sure there was a war and there was fighting and killing, but there was also a faithful sense of duty to your fellow men: a kind of unconditional love. George wasn't alone, hundreds and hundreds of boats came to our aid. They say there were six hundred and ninety-three in total.'

'That's the number on your arm.'

'It's a *very* special number.'

'But I bet there was a mad race down to the shore when those boats arrived?' says Jason, entranced by the splendour of the image of his boats, picturing the rescue in his head, swept away by the sight of them over the water.

'I expect there were plenty of fights, weren't there, with everybody trying to jump in and scramble their way to safety?'

'If there was any fighting I didn't see it. Everyone waited their turn as far as I can remember.'

'And were there enough boats for everyone?'

'No, many were left behind. They tried to escape over land instead.

We mustn't forget those protecting the coastline from land invasion either – the rear-guard, holding back the attack whilst we climbed aboard the boats – lining up four and five deep across the dunes, staying behind to give the rest of us a chance of survival.'

'What happened to them?'

Arnold grips the photo tightly. 'We would have done the same for them if it had been our job to stay there, Jason. We will never forget them.'

Jason looks out of the window. Outside everything seems suddenly tame and meaningless. 'I'm sorry about your friends,' he whispers. 'It must be hard to forget, to carry on.'

'I shall *never* forget, sonny. I shall remember them to my dying day. But you must understand, it is because of ordinary men, brave men, just like these,' and he clutches the photo tightly, 'that *you* cannot give in. You and I have a duty to make their sacrifice worthwhile.'

'So do you go to church and stuff now?' asks Jason, noticing a thin bamboo cross standing on the mantelpiece behind the letter rack, tucked in amongst a small vase of artificial flowers.

'I think *I* probably would after all that. And what about God? Do you believe he exists? And the sea, are you afraid of going back there since … well … I mean is the beach a sad place for you?'

Arnold frowns, rubs his chin with his forefinger. 'That's a great many questions sonny, a great many. When you're faced with what we were faced with, you will believe in *anything* to survive.

God was in a great many men's hearts on that beach, I can tell you, men who had never set foot in a church, men who had never considered the possibility of there even *being* a deity before that day.

But to me, the sense of comradeship and loyalty we felt was the only religion I needed.

In answer to your questions no, I don't go to church, but not a day goes by when I don't think about what I went through and what those other poor souls endured, those who weren't as lucky as I was. The beach holds many memories for me but I haven't been back there. It's a long way and it would be a lonely journey for a widower.

The past has gone and we should learn from it. Then we must move on, though I know we shall never be able to repay those men in their boats who saved our lives. They will live in here for the rest of my days,' he says, placing his hand on his heart.

'Is that why you have a picture of a boat on your arm?'

'We all had one,' Arnold smiles, pointing to the photo. 'To remember.'

PART NINE

Mary is stuffing a turkey in the kitchen when Seamus casually announces he is leaving.

'Going anywhere nice?' Jason asks indifferently, one eye on the television.

'I mean for good.'

'Oh, right.' Jason doesn't care whether Seamus stays or otherwise. There doesn't seem any point saying much else on the matter.

Early the following morning, Jason watches as Seamus packs up a few belongings before driving off to his sister's house on the south coast in the same battered car he brought Jason back from the Home in all those years ago.

'If you must know, I've 'ad just about enough of you and them blasted twins ... and she's nowt but a lazy naggin' cow,' Seamus mutters as he starts the engine to leave.

It's taken you long enough to work that out, Jason thinks, smiling, just as Mary appears at the upstairs window.

'Good riddance to bad rubbish,' she shrieks, 'hope you rot in hell,' and she looks down to see Jason standing at the front door wearing oversized grey pyjamas and a bemused expression. 'I'll wipe that smile off your face too, scumbag,' she screams. 'You're *out*. Hear me? I'm gonna make sure you go somewhere as far away from 'ere as possible. Money'll be tight now Seamus 'as beggared off and left me single again, and you're not gettin' the chance to eat me and the twins out of 'ouse and 'ome.'

'You can't get rid,' goads Jason from a respectable distance, the twins appearing in the doorway next to him. 'I'm not sixteen 'til August and you're my legal guardian 'til then ... so dream on.'

The twins cower in the doorframe, infected by the aggressive tone of his voice, their small round faces pale and fearful.

'Don't worry, kids,' Jason mutters, before turning to go back into the house, 'you've only got another fourteen years before you're free of her.'

As soon as Seamus goes, Mary slops downstairs in the grubby faded T-shirt she wears as a nightie, hair scraped back into an unruly bun, hollow skin dragged taught around her eyes and cheeks. She misses breakfast completely, lighting a cigarette from the stove as she impatiently tops up the twin's beakers with yesterday's yellowing milk. Then she goes to the bottom stair in the hallway, sits down next to the telephone table and begins to thumb noisily through the phone book like some agitated maniac in need of medication, making call after call. And then, not getting the answers she wants, she slams the receiver down with mighty thuds, yelling hysterically at the twins if they so much as dare peep around the corner.

Jason stays out of her way.

He feels sorry for Rory and Beth but they are not his responsibility, and if he starts spending too much time with them Mary will come to expect his help around the place more and more.

But he knows she's up to something.

By lunchtime she is on her second pack of cigarettes and an air of peace has descended.

'You can pack your bags,' she says blankly, 'I've got you in at Boulton.'

'Never heard of it,' Jason replies, warily, watching her as she wipes nicotine stained hands repeatedly up and down her T-shirt, a languid feline grin on her face.

'It's a boarding school – for scum like you. And it's a long way from here, so there's no chance of you coming grovelling at my door again.'

The number forty stops at six-eighteen each morning at the end of Furnace Street. It's always empty at that time of the day, save for the odd night worker dozing on the backseat.

Jason drags a tatty suitcase and threadbare rucksack up onto the luggage shelf and takes the first seat behind the driver. Even Mary has got up early, left the twins asleep, and come to make sure he gets on the bus.

'And don't think I want you knocking on my door in the holidays either,' she yells from the pavement as Jason stares out through the dirty window, 'because you'll not be welcome back 'ere again.'

'Don't worry,' he mouths through the condensation and grime, 'I'd rather die than spend another day in your house. I never want to see you again, crabby old witch.'

It is the longest single sentence he has ever shared with Mary … and quite possibly his favourite.

'Sister or mother?' asks the bus driver as they set off.

'Neither. Just a nobody.'

And that's the last he ever sees of or hears from his guardian.

Jason sits back in his seat. He leans against the glass and looks vacantly out of the window. A smell of warm diesel washes over him

'Where you headin',' lad?'

'Boulton,' Jason replies, the name igniting a spark causing him to jump up suddenly from his seat and sprint for the door, grabbing his bags on the way.

'Drop me here will you? I've got something to do first before I go.'

Number eleven looks much the same as always.

The gate needs oiling but he won't get the chance now. Jason sighs irritably and knocks on the front door.

'What a pleasant surprise, please come in.'

'I'm just coming to say goodbye. I'm … I'm leaving for Boulton Academy today.' Jason blurts the words out clumsily.

There is a silence. Arnold turns and walks away down the hallway towards the kitchen.

Jason follows him. This visit could be like any other visit, and yet it feels so different. Jason's heart is heavy, his head adrift with wild thoughts. It's starting to feel like it used to feel, when the rage enveloped him, when the blind panic overtook his emotions.

What if Boulton turns out to be like The Home, or like Leicester Road? What then?

'Keep the door closed, sonny – that's right – don't want all this nice warm air escaping.'

Arnold leans down to light the gas fire and then turns to face Jason.

'That's grand, really it is. Boulton is a wonderful place – I'm sure you'll do very well there.'

But Jason's stomach churns and plummets because he cannot believe the old man today.

'Do you think so? Do you mean that?'

'It has an excellent reputation.'

'For who, no-hopers?'

'For anyone who wants to succeed – it doesn't matter where you've come from, sonny – it's what you do from now on that matters. The point is … you *will* get a chance to make something of yourself at Boulton, so don't waste that chance.

The future is in your hands, the past is gone, cannot be altered.

But it's a very strict place from what I've heard, so you'll have to look sharp and show them what you're made of. You'll have to shape up and do as you are told, no bunking off or giving cheek. Now then, I'll just go and put the kettle on, shall I?'

Jason sits down in an easy chair and looks around the room.

He will miss all this.

He presses his fingernails into the palms of his hands.

By the time Arnold returns with the tea tray, Jason's palms are marked red and his throat stretched so tight with fear he can't speak properly.

'It's okay, lad,' says Arnold, placing the tea tray in front of Jason, 'I do understand. Nobody likes change – but you're strong, you'll cope. Trust me. It will be fine this time.'

But the tea tastes funny to Jason and he can hardly swallow.

'I … I've not felt like this for ages,' he manages at last. 'I think it's just … just …'

'It's just nerves, just a young man understandably finding his circumstances a little trying. I'd be the same in your shoes – believe me. But you can conquer this, Jason, you really can. *You* are in control now. I know you are ready to do this. I have every confidence in you.'

Then Arnold stands up, rolls up his sleeves and holds his hands palm-side up in front of his face.

'Hit me!'

'What? Are you mad?'

'Go on, show me what you're made of.' Arnold begins to dance around Jason's chair, sparring with fresh air, teasing him into throwing a punch.

'Don't. Please don't.' Jason puts his hands over his face.

'Come on, sonny, show me how you do it, come on.
You're supposed to be a fighter, aren't you? Don't tell me
you're chicken – Jason King – too scared to hit an old man.'
Arnold is having fun. His old body skips and hops in old
worn slippers that seem to slide across the patterned kitchen
carpet.

'This is crazy,' Jason announces at last. 'I'm *not* going
to hit you.'

'Why?' asks Arnold, panting.

'Because I don't want to, because you're my friend.'

Arnold rolls down his shirtsleeves and nods. 'See? It's
all up to you – the future and what you do with it. You don't
have to fight anymore. You have a choice. You're no longer
out of control, Jason. You're winning your battle against all
the hatred and the fear and the despair.'

Then Arnold turns and goes out of the room leaving
Jason alone to finish his tea.

But Jason is not quite alone. He is in the company of the
spirits who see everything, say nothing and who smile down
at him from above, in the knowledge that it shouldn't be too
long now.

The driver peers at Jason through the mirror on the front
windscreen of the bus. 'Which stop, lad?'

'Don't know. It's called Boulton Academy.'

'Right you are. I'll give you a nod.'

The rhythmic throb of the engine lulls Jason to sleep.
The next thing he knows a voice reaches out across the void
of emptiness in his head.

'Wake up. This is your stop.'

Jason jumps up, still half asleep, and ambles down the
bus to collect his baggage. The driver leans out of his chair
and salutes him. 'Take it easy, my friend.'

'Yeah. Whatever,' replies Jason, stepping down onto the pavement.

Outside, the freshness hits him. It's a welcome change from the suffocating heat of the bus and Jason pulls his shirt collar away from his damp neck in an effort to cool down.

Grasses sway this way and that in the breeze; a tropical sun filters through tall trees lining the roadside, breaking through in sudden flashes then disappearing again until the next time.

Slinging his rucksack onto one shoulder, Jason picks up his suitcase with the other before scanning both ways up and down the road.

'Blast! Should have asked which way to go,' he grumbles, 'still, this is a bit of all right. I wish Tom were here, we could lift some handy gear.'

Huge houses line the roadside, protected by long driveways and carefully tended gardens. Silent men in green boiler suits mow straight lines up and down bowling green lawns where cleverly illuminated water fountains cascade into perfectly circular ponds.

Jason sets off towards a church steeple, for no other reason than it's a landmark and it stands out like a beacon amongst the roof tops and towering oaks and elms.

A car approaches from behind, accelerating throatily as it passes, making Jason jump. 'Moron!' he shouts.

Soon the road begins to climb and wind. Jason's breathing quickens with the effort of carrying his load and his hair begins to stick to the nape of his neck again.

Just as the novelty of walking under the gaze of the blistering sun begins to wear thin, a van slows down and stops a little way in front of Jason. Instinctively he runs towards it. When he reaches the passenger side, a head leans out.

'Want a lift?'

'Thanks, yeah.' Jason pushes his bags onto a shelf in the back before hopping in beside the driver.

'Where you heading?'

'Boulton Academy.'

'That's handy. Me too.'

'You live there?'

'Nope, got a delivery for them. Then I'm off home. Going on holiday tomorrow. Me and the missus and my little lad.'

'Anywhere nice?'

'Scotland. June loves it. Folks were Scottish. Both dead now, but she likes to go back and see the old haunts when she can. And it's pretty – by the sea – nice pub and all that. Getting harder now we've got the little one. Long journey see, but he's a good lad.'

Jason nods, settling back into his seat.

'How old is your kid then?'

'Three last month – going to be a real star when he grows up, mark my words. He'll make something of himself, he will – make me and his Mum really proud one day, not that we're not proud of him already – but you know what I mean. You looking forward to going to Boulton?'

Jason shrugs. 'Not sure, do you know what it's like?'

'Not really, I just go in with deliveries now and again Everyone seems friendly enough though.'

It is a far cry from Furnace Street.

Like a cross between a grandiose stately home and a concentration camp, Boulton Academy is a rambling monument of a building set in acres and acres of grounds and surrounded by extensive meadows and woodland.

A tall silent boy with a thin, flat mouth meets Jason in the hallway and leads him, briskly, to his bedroom.

The room is large with a high ceiling and recessed window that overlooks the enormous gardens. There are two single beds made up. Jason makes for the one nearest the window, throwing his rucksack and suitcase onto it before jumping on it himself.

Reclining against the bed-head, legs crossed and arms behind his head, he whistles at his good fortune.

This place isn't half bad, he thinks, in fact it's like a bloody hotel!

He looks at his watch.

Ten past three.

He's probably missed lunch.

Feeling in the front pocket of his rucksack, Jason pulls out a bar of chocolate and breaks it into double chunks, eating quickly before wiping his mouth with the back of his sleeve and then wandering into the little bathroom in search of something to drink. He fills the toothbrush beaker with water from the bath and drinks it.

There is a firm knock on the bedroom door. Jason opens it and peers out onto the landing.

'Dr Knopfler would like to see you now.'

The messenger shows no inclination towards friendliness.

'But I've not eaten yet – only some chocolate – and I need to unpack my things.'

'This isn't a hotel. I said *now*.'

It's not the same boy Jason met when he first arrived. This one looks a little older, broad and muscular, and he glares impatiently at Jason.

'Right, right, keep your hair on, I'm coming …This Dr Knopfler guy … is he the boss?'

The other boy nods, curtly, as they walk briskly down a long carpeted corridor. A bubble of indignation rises in

Jason's chest. You could at least talk to me, you ignorant sod, he thinks, sourly.

Once inside Dr Knopfler's office, Jason steals a second or two to look around.

The room is sparsely furnished.

Good job I'm not still on the make, Jason smiles. There's nothing here worth nicking.

'You must be Jason King,' a voice snaps suddenly, a thin bespectacled man appearing in the doorway. Sunlight reflects lazily on his shiny head from the window behind as he licks and twirls a wet moustache into a curled bayonet.

'I would like to welcome you to our fine establishment, if I may. And I must begin by telling you, Mr King, that we expect very high standards from all our pupils. We do *not* tolerate idleness or cheek here. You have been sent to Boulton for one reason and one reason only. Do you have any idea what that reason might be?'

Because Mary wanted rid, Jason thinks, silently, at the same time shaking his head dimly.

'Self improvement through discipline.'

It means nothing to Jason. He slams his hands deep into his trouser pockets and stares at the floor.

Dr Knopfler slopes towards Jason, stooping slightly, arms clasped behind his back.

Jason looks up. He is mesmerised by the moustache. It begins to unravel in front of his eyes.

'Well? Have you a tongue in your head?'

'Yes, of course I have,' smiles Jason, jumping to attention.

'Yes, *Sir* – at this school you reply yes, *Sir* – understand?'

'Yes ... Yes, *Sir!*'

'Discipline!' continues Dr Knopfler, circling slowly around Jason like a lion might circle its prey. 'In this school we demand *discipline* and *honesty* and *hard-work.*'

'Yes! … Sir!'

'And I want to see you at lessons bright and early in the morning. Pupils who come here from other schools are usually lazy or slow or rude.

You will need to work hard if you are to stay – you will do well to remember that.'

Jason goes to bed that night feeling his world is being ripped apart.

He will give it a few days, test the water, and if things don't improve he'll think of a way of getting out.

He won't go back to Mary's – she wouldn't have him anyway – and he'll be sixteen next birthday, so he'll be able to do what the hell he likes then.

Lying on his back, staring at the ceiling, he wills himself to sleep, drifting in and out of a fitful slumber until a new day dawns and sharp rasps of morning light filter through the curtains to rouse him.

Things do improve. As the weeks pass by, the uncertainty of those first few days becomes no more than a hazy memory.

Jason forgets about wanting to leave Boulton.

He settles into the rigorous routine, like a cog in a spectacular piece of machinery that grinds unyieldingly, stretching its workers to the limit, and he discovers quickly and willingly what is expected of him. Jason relishes the rigidity of this new life with its stiff indomitable boundaries, like well-defined cursors, inflexibly demanding and yet ultimately rewarding.

All pupils at Boulton wake at the same time, dress in identical uniforms, eat their meals together, tidy their rooms simultaneously and arrive for lessons in quiet, organised lines.

Lessons are from nine until two, five days a week, with a short break for lunch. There then follows a strict regime of physical exercise until five-thirty, after which the boys eat and are encouraged to take part in extra-curricular disciplines such as rugby, cross-country, survival techniques, fitness training.

Jason's new life is like a well-oiled instrument, precise and unwavering, and for that he is thankful.

He needs the meticulous predictability that each day at Boulton brings, like the rising sun and the ebbing tide.

Weekends at Boulton mean sport.

Jason has never excelled at physical exercise before. He always felt excluded at his other schools; team games were never his thing, other team members rarely his allies.

But at Boulton, solitude is never scorned and Jason finds himself drawn to lonely pursuits that feed his independent spirit and self-reliant nature – long distance running, swimming ... but mostly climbing.

Saturday is climbing day.

Returning from the climbing wall one Saturday afternoon, Jason swings open the door to his room and throws his damp sweatshirt onto the bed. As he runs a bath, he hums a throwaway tune and strips off the rest of his clothes, leaving them in a heap on the floor, whilst steam froths lightly from the bathroom and clouds the room.

'Well, well, well!' pierces through the foggy haze. It is coming from the easy chair by the window next to Jason's bed.

'So it really *is* you?'

It is more of an assertion than a question.

'Who's that?' Jason snaps.

'I'm surprised you've kept out of trouble this long. Still, we can always change that, can't we? Thought you'd be inside by now, under lock and key. You always were a loose cannon, and stupid too, from what I remember...'

PART TEN

'Who's there?' Jason snaps again from the bowels of the bathroom, hurriedly turning off the hot tap, snatching a bath towel from the back of a chair and wrapping it around his waist.

He squints, but can't quite make out the face that accompanies the voice, even though it's oddly familiar – like an annoying song he's heard and yet can't quite remember the name of the singer – and he strains desperately to focus in the steamy half-light.

'You must have known I'd find you one day, King; hunt you out and give you what you deserve? I always said I would – and I *always* keep my promises.'

'Stefan? ... Stefan, is that you?' Realisation grips Jason with a surge of panic.

'Jesus, Stefan! What are you doing here? How the hell did you get in to *my* room?'

'*Our* room ... there isn't another free. But if I'd known you were here I'd have refused it, slept in the car until they could find me another one,' he spits, acidly. 'Much as I've looked forward to our meeting again, I have no inclination to share a room with you.'

Jason grips the towel tightly around his waist with one hand and clenches the knuckles on his free hand.

The urge is still there. It alarms him. He can't – not here – not now he's beginning to fit in for the first time in his life. Even if Stefan provokes him like he did in the old days, even if he twists himself into Jason's head and fills his mind with doubt and despair, Jason has just *got* to keep in control.

Stefan Barzel is *not* going to ruin everything, not this time, thinks Jason defiantly. I've got a right to be here. I'm no second-rate loser, whatever you think. I'm making something of my life and that's how it's going to stay.

Forcing a deep breath Jason cultivates an unconvincing smile. 'Well then, we'll just have to make the best of it, won't we?'

Stefan snorts and drags the back of his hand across his nose like a violin bow. 'Not bloody likely, I suggest you keep out of my way, King. I mean it. Ruin this for me and you'll live to regret it. That is … if you live at all.'

The following Saturday, Jason collects a helmet and harness from the storeroom as usual and makes his way to the larger of the two gyms to practise on the climbing wall.

He's waited all week for this moment.

The discomfort of meeting Stefan again, the mental anguish of having to share a room with him makes this an absolute lifeline, like a red-hot date he's waited all week to arrange.

But Stefan is there when Jason arrives, high up in the eaves, swinging below the rafters, his orange helmet a warning beacon above Jason's head.

Stefan looks down and sees Jason peering up. 'Let's see how good you are then, King. I've heard you fancy yourself as a bit of a climber?'

Stefan abseils effortlessly down to where Jason is standing. Unbuckling his harness, he lets it clatter to the floor around his ankles. 'Makes it more interesting this way,' he says, laughing, absently tightening his gloves.

'We're not allowed to climb unaided.' Jason tries to calm the tremor in his voice. 'There's a sign in the entrance hall. We must *always* wear a harness.'

Stefan stiffens slightly, as though about to say something, but then his body relaxes and he lets out an audible sigh, giving Jason a flash of that old derisive smile, at the same time glancing a sideways look up to the tiny platform at the top of the wall.

'Well, if you're not up to it ...'

It's all the encouragement Jason needs and he has his foot planted firmly on the first foothold before Stefan finishes his sentence.

This will be the end of it one way or another. All the unfinished business between them that so obviously still rankles like a bitter pill in Stefan's head will be absolved once and for all – as soon as Jason reaches the top that is, triumphant, jubilant, all conquering.

And soon they are both close to the platform in the eaves of the gym where it is cold and vast with nothing but steel rafters to break a fall.

Jason hopes none of the masters come in and see him climbing without a harness.

He will be in big trouble.

They both will be.

Perhaps that is why he loses his handhold – too busy worrying, trying to get the climb done with before he gets found out – and before he has time to think he is hanging on with one hand, tendons bulging with the effort of carrying the full weight of his body, feet trembling, with the sheer effort of hanging on.

He swings a leg out. It causes him to sway across the face of the wall. Then he lunges towards the hard grey crater-like surface with his free hand.

Finding the hold he is fumbling so desperately for, he pushes heavily into the wall with all his weight, hugging it to his trembling body, fighting for his life. He is unable to move again until the burning fear in his throat subsides, before the throbbing in his temples dies away and he can advance, gingerly, to the platform.

Stefan is already there. He is fastening himself into a harness.

'Where did you get that from?' Jason cries.

'Didn't you know, King? You're not allowed to climb without one.'

'You devious b …'

' … You not got one? Oh dear. And there only seems to be this one.'

Stefan pivots round until he is standing square in front of Jason. He flicks the thick rope of the harness into Jason's face. The rope snaps into Jason's cheek and sends him flailing onto his knees.

The platform is narrow, the ground far, far below and the wall casts gloomy shadows across the gym like some inexplicable vortex spiralling into the depths and out of sight.

Jason steadies himself and shuffles back into the centre of the platform, level with Stefan's knees.

He is conscious of blood trickling from his cheek, dripping onto the wooden plinth of the platform, but he daren't risk letting go with one hand to wipe it away.

He is aware of Stefan's foot jerking up, but he is not fast enough to move out of the way and it stamps down on the back of his hand.

The platform judders, wobbles precariously and then settles itself again.

'Enough,' whispers Jason. 'I've had enough … what's it all about Stefan? Can't you just let it go?'

'It's about *you* – it's always been about *you* – that's the whole point. You ruined The Home for everyone – you're a loser, King – the rest of us never got any attention – it was always you, you, you …

You'd hit one of us and they would spend all day in meetings deciding how to punish you. Or you would run away and they'd be hours looking for you. How do you think it was for the rest of us? Us who were normal? Shoved in front of the telly for hours like we didn't matter, whilst they sorted *you* – the bloody freak – out.'

'But *you* made me what I am – you and the others – you wouldn't leave me alone. You never left me alone, never.' Jason's mind is spinning with memories.

Stefan shakes his head. 'You forced me to do it in the end, King. You were no more than an attention seeking little scumbag ... and nothing's changed from what I can see. But you're not going to ruin it for me again ... I can promise you that much.'

Jason looks up and meets Stefan's crazed gaze. 'Stop talking crap. Nobody neglected you. You were spoilt at that place. Let's face it, you were hardly virgin white yourself.'

'Meaning?'

'The bullying, the name calling, the threats of what you'd do to me if I told them you were hitting me and making me steal for you. Do you want me to go on?'

Stefan nods. 'Yes. Say it!'

'Say it? Say what? Haven't I said enough? I can't see how you think you were neglected. They all worshipped you – you couldn't do a thing wrong – and you were always in Miss Lemon's room at night. How cushy was that? And what went on in there ... pervert ... don't imagine I didn't realise what she was doing, the dirty cow.'

A smirk slowly crosses Stefan's face as though he's been told a joke some time ago and has only just fully understood the punch line.

'Do you know what?'

Jason frowns and shakes his head. 'What?'

'You really *don't* know what I'm talking about, do you? I always knew you weren't the sharpest knife in the drawer, but you're even more stupid than I ever imagined,' he says, spreading his arms wide. 'You couldn't ruin it for me at The

Home, could you, you couldn't tell anyone – couldn't spill the beans back then – because you had absolutely no idea what I'd done?'

'You're off your head,' Jason drawls, slackening his grip on the sides of the platform and spitting blood from between his gums. 'But you're right – I have no idea what you're going on about. Just tell me and we can end this stupid game.'

'I didn't know it would end like it did,' Stefan says calmly, 'but once I felt the knife sink in, I just carried on and on ... and do you know what? I enjoyed it. And it was all because of *you* ... nobody else ... just *you*. If you'd told them about Miss Lemon, about the way she treated her favourites, and that stealing the food was my idea, it would have ruined my reputation, it would have ruined everything in fact. They all thought I was perfect, see, destined for great things. I was right to set you up, to lay the blame on you. You didn't twig at all, did you?'

'You?' Jason can barely part with the accusation, forcing it through clenched teeth, contempt etched across his features in gauged lines of hatred.

Stefan sniggers. 'Brain dead, that's what you were – still are probably. I had to get rid of you then and now it looks like I'm going to have to do it all over again.'

The words filter absurdly into Jason's tremulous consciousness.

'So ... so it *was* you? You? *You* did it. It was nothing to do with me?'

Stefan laughs, shoulders rocking helplessly, whilst all Jason can do is look on.

'You ruddy low life. You bloody evil son of a ...'

'You took your time, King. Surely you can see that I couldn't risk you staying. I had to get rid of you to make sure you didn't blab. Can't believe you didn't catch on sooner.

Anyone else would have worked it out years ago. And now you know the truth, I can't risk you blabbing again.'

Jason swallows hard and tries to take a tentative step towards Stefan.

'Go on then, King! Take a swipe. Don't fancy your chances up here. Oh dear,' he simpers, sickeningly, looking down at the ground far, far below, 'too bad you aren't wearing a harness.'

Jason's breath is coming in shallow gulps.

He's felt this way too often before.

Most lately that night when Seamus hit him so hard that his nose cracked and splintered.

And it's happening to him now, that imaginary sound in his ears of bone crunching against flesh, the fermenting abyss of crazed aggression desperate to burst through in an act of furious retaliation. It would be so easy. Too easy. He'd be justified too, wouldn't he?

But it would ruin everything for Jason and that's what Stefan wants so badly.

Jason must resist, stay true – he has to focus on remaining calm.

Disorientated, he stumbles, in a moment of dizziness, reaching out to Stefan.

Stefan pushes him away roughly, but in doing so he loses his balance and tumbles over the edge of the platform, catching his foot in the harness rope as he falls.

Fifteen feet below them, the rope snags on an overhang and breaks Stefan's fall, but his helmet makes a sharp crunch as his head hits the wall and he is left upside down and motionless, suspended in mid air, rotating around and around whilst the thick jute rope untwists.

Although every fibre in Jason's body tells him to leave Stefan where he is, to take this opportunity for revenge a strange voice in his head pleads for compassion. He reacts with lightning speed. Climbing down Stefan's own rope, he unties the loop that has become snagged around Stefan's foot, before clasping himself into Stefan's harness and hauling Stefan's inert form over his shoulder and descending to the ground.

Stefan should feel lucky. If the rope hadn't snagged and Jason hadn't been there to assist him, he would most surely be dead now. So why does Jason feel it is his own luck that is in question when Stefan is due to return to Boulton after a short stay in hospital?

He sits on the chair by the window in his bedroom, looking forward to Stefan's return like a three-legged donkey would look forward to a visit from a half-starved lion.

A breeze wafts across his face – as cool as pebbles in a river – but his skin feels clammy and his heart strangely unsettled.

The memory of that fateful day with Stefan is now no more than an unsteady recollection that flits in and out of his thoughts, like a moth tapping aimlessly against the window pane, but the realisation that he could have actually died trying to save Stefan's life nags at him with a jarring dissent.

Why did I help him in the first place?

Good deeds aren't generally my thing.

Hell, if the boot had been on the other foot, Stefan would have left me to die, of that there is no doubt. And, if Stefan had fallen a hundred or so feet to his death, I wouldn't be sitting here now ... staring out into space, wishing I were somewhere else and he wasn't coming back.

'I can't go on like this,' Jason says, out of the blue, even though there is nobody else in the room.

He gets up and puts on his jacket, studies his reflection in the bathroom mirror and is surprised to discover he likes what he sees.

'I'm not a victim anymore,' he says, massaging his temples with the tips of his fingers. 'Arnold was right. I *am* in control. Stefan cannot hurt me. I know that much. Maybe he will let it go, re-evaluate what is important in his life, make a fresh start and leave me to get on with mine ...'

Two days later Stefan sits on Jason's favourite chair by the window, right leg in plaster, supported by an old footstool.

Jason enters the room.

'You okay?'

'Leave it, King.'

'Just thought maybe we could call it quits, start afresh, you know – after everything. Maybe we should move on? We're both stuck here, aren't we ... in the same college ... same lessons ... same room?'

There is a half smile on Stefan's face. 'I'm past making a fresh start. Coming back here with this ruddy thing on my leg is bad enough. Besides, we have old business to finish before I can *move on* – as you so sweetly put it. Your schoolboy heroics haven't changed a thing.'

Jason studies Stefan's profile from the doorway.

He has never taken much notice before but now, as the sun trickles through the window, it casts brilliant colour on Stefan's cheeks and Jason can see how fabulously ugly he really is, face drawn and wretched, it could have been created by a blunt axe, deliciously devoid of compassion and feeling.

'Are you still going on the outward bound course next weekend with you being laid up like that?' Jason asks, nodding towards the shiny metal crutches draped across the arm of Stefan's chair, desperately hoping the answer will be no.

Stefan rolls his eyes and turns away, stares out of the window into the gardens beyond. 'Leave me alone, King. Get out – you're getting on my nerves.'

Jason takes it as a yes.

Their destination is two hours away from Boulton by coach.

Jason is tired.

He hasn't slept well since Stefan's return earlier in the week, lying in the dark night after night, unable to block out the overwhelming gloom brought on by Stefan's rhythmic breathing.

Jason yawns and folds his sweater into a cushion shape before wedging it against the window on the back seat. Dozing off, his mind drifts to the sea and the sand, to boats afloat on calm blue waters, and he wakes with a jolt to find a breeze streaming in through the partially opened window.

He inhales the unmistakable perfume of salt water and sand and wipes the condensation from the window with his bare arm, straining to see outside.

There is a beach to one side. It stretches out along a wide coastline with mottled headlands in the distance. And there are boats in the bay, all firmly anchored, bobbing on the spot with masts flinching, jingling and clinking, soothing Jason's anxious mind. He can just make out the top of Stefan's head on a seat near the front of the coach. If only the sea could calm his rage, too, thinks Jason, wistfully. If only it were that simple.

I'm here, he sighs, contentedly, as the coach draws to a halt. I'm home again.

Outside gulls circle under the grey vault sky and Jason's flesh pulses with each cry. It's been a long time. Too long.

Jason is first off the coach, reeling in enormous shoals of sea air, lost in dreams amongst the waves.

Later that evening, alone and with a sense of renewed peace and hope, Jason heads for the shore.

It is eight-thirty and the sun is sinking below the watery horizon.

He wanders along the edge of the gently lapping waves, hands in pockets, looking out at the boats in the dusky light, counting them, wishing he could reach out and touch them.

Everyone else is inside, but I had to come here. I have to see this again – to feel it and be a part of it – it's been too long.

Eventually Jason turns back in the direction of the dunes, just as the moon tips behind a cloud and plunges them into darkness.

When it re-emerges some seconds later, the beach is aglow in its blue after-light and Stefan Barzel is standing on the path, barring Jason's way with his crutches, a vile sneer crossing his lips. 'Having a nice stroll?'

'You've been drinking.'

'And?'

'Get out of my way, Barzel. You're tragic. I don't fight paraplegics.' Jason laughs out loud with the recklessness of it all: the beach, the dunes and because of Stefan Barzel, leaning on two shiny crutches, body stooped – disillusioned into believing he still has the power to frighten Jason.

'What's so funny, King? Find it amusing that I've got these bloody useless things?' And he waves his crutches in the air.

Jason ducks.

Stefan hunches closer. 'What I'd like to do to that smug face of yours, King ...'

Jason sucks in the salty air and stands tall in the half-light of the watching moon. 'Leave it. Just leave it! Sod off back inside. I'm not interested. It's all in the past. *I've* moved on and so should you.'

'Oh, I *will* move on, you can be sure of that, just as soon as I have done what I set out to do.' Stefan's voice is threatening and there's danger in his eyes.

Then Jason says nothing for a while, letting the ebb and flow of the evening tide settle the palpitations that heave angrily against his chest, before turning his back on Stefan and silently walking away down the beach.

'Hey! Don't you dare walk away from me! *Nobody* turns their back on me.' And Stefan hurls a crutch at Jason's back.

It lands with a dull thud on the sand beside Jason.

He turns calmly and picks it up, holding it at arm's length, offering it back to Stefan.

'I'm going back now,' Jason murmurs, quietly, 'you can stay out here all night, but *I* want to go to sleep.'

The first punch lands rib hard on Jason's stomach.

He doubles up, clutching his abdomen.

Stefan's laughter reverberates across the dunes as he swings for a second time, this time with his crutch, slamming it down on the back of Jason's neck, forcing him to the ground like a stone slab.

'No! Please! For God's sake … no more, it's … it's over.'

'Over?' shrieks Stefan, excitedly, 'I think you'll find it's only just beginning. I was *born* to hate you, King, and *hate* you is exactly what I'm going to do. You were a loser when we were kids … you'll *always* be a loser. I may as well finish the job now, once and for all.'

The final blow crunches into Jason across the right side of his face with the impending force of an axe cracking a log in two.

A sound of shattering bone echoes through Jason's head long after the impact sends him plummeting onto the sand.

There is no chance of retaliation anymore.

Jason sprawls helplessly on the ground, powerless to resist. He can barely sense Stefan's presence looming over him, and Stefan prods him with his crutch like a cat toying with an injured bird.

'That all you can take, soft lad? Guess I'll leave you here then. Sweet dreams.' And Stefan limps away down the path, leaving Jason in the dark.

The dark does not frighten him any more.

It is not like it was in the cellar: cold, damp and Jason fearful with the promise of more punishment to come.

This is a place of escape.

Besides, Jason can smell the sand and the sea, so there is no need to be afraid.

Could this be some kind of blissful homecoming?

Paradise?

Everything feels unreal, blurred. Jason tries to move but he can't. His shattered body slides deeper into the damp sand with every writhe and twitch.

They find him in the dunes the next morning, enshrined by the tall swaying grasses and fine gritty sand. The paramedics are called but Jason is pronounced dead at the scene.

His body is taken away, lain to rest until it can be dug deep into the ground, left to rot, its earthly task finished. But nobody kneels and cries beside his coffin, nobody grieves for Jason King.

It seems a soul without love is a lonely soul and a soul without love still cannot find a place in the Heavenly House.

PART ELEVEN

It is six o'clock in the morning.

Already Jason can tell by the heat of the sun that it is going to be another scorcher.

They have to get going soon; have to reach Cassel by dusk tomorrow, for these are the orders.

He cannot remember what day it is.

Everything is just one endless grind, one long painful creep across fields and roads, through villages and farms. The odd thing is he doesn't remember getting into this mess in the first place. The past seems unreal, blurred.

And they all stopped talking days ago. Any excitement they felt soon fizzled out – jokes, banter – all eventually trickling to nothing as the days became longer and longer, food supply smaller … no water, no rest, no sense of humour left.

Jason's feet are raw from wearing the same socks and badly fitting boots for many days. He complained about those boots months ago, they weren't his size then and they're certainly not his size now – too small – but it all seems unimportant in the searing heat. He has angry blisters that rub against the cracked dry leather until they weep, wounds infected with dust and mud and grit from the continual pounding on the polluted roads.

Men are falling along the way.

Jason can sense who will be next.

It's becoming a game, a charade to pass a few dreary hours. Always the same old pattern.

Trembling legs, forced to carry an exhausted body with no will left to survive, the same legs that eventually grind to barely a shuffle, ploughing through clay and mud and decaying excrement, too weak to carry on, too exhausted to care.

But Jason cannot give in, he won't allow it.

A steely determination drives him towards the coast – a simmering resolve that directs him towards the sea and the sand and the rushing clouds that head for home ... and England.

Hours pass.

They keep on walking.

There seems to be no end.

Maybe there isn't.

A resigned silence echoes in time to the marching feet. Eventually they reach a squalid farmstead.

'Hey, lads,' shouts a chirpy voice from down the ranks. 'I got me some lovely fish and chips over here. Vinegar anyone?'

Jason manages a weakly smile.

Men are peering into a filthy dustbin by the roadside. A loaf of bread is hauled out from the bottom. Even from a distance Jason can see it is green and blotched with mould.

'Here we are then, tuck in one and all.'

Much later, as the sun fades and the air becomes less oppressive, Jason feels the closeness of the sea, smells the salt around him, hears the distant comforting siren of seagulls. His pace quickens and, desperately, he grits his teeth with the dizzy anticipation of what he might find when he reaches the coast.

'Not far now, boys, keep it up. Only another twenty miles or so ...'

Night-time comes and goes. The sky is overcast. Still they trudge onward.

Clouds of black smoke hang in the air like silk, drifting aimlessly, spiralling skywards, whilst bombs fall and planes rumble overhead.

Snipers on street corners take their forbidden chances, whilst tanks hidden in farmyards under piles of straw flank left and take aim.

Another scorching day ends. They finally arrive in Cassel. Much fewer in number than when they set out, sleeping where they drop in the marketplace – next to the clock tower or in the shadow of the trees lining the roadside – anywhere they feel safe and out of sight.

But Jason can't sleep.

He is too close now to think about sleeping.

Gulls scream overhead, telling him that the sea is there, stretching towards him like a mother might reach out for her child, screeching for him to hang on, not to give up.

Jason looks up at the moon, a vibrant blue orb that wraps an ironically reassuring glow over the village marketplace, and he imagines it casting the same light over the sea … and over England.

They set off next morning in the half-light of dawn, thinning khaki lines, streaming murderously onward to reach the coast before the Germans realise they are on the move again.

Jason can hear crying as he walks, whimpers of injured men huddled by the sides of the road, some pleading not to be left, others past caring, too near death to notice.

Jason concentrates his gaze on the horizon.

He cannot afford to look at them.

They are all like me – just like me – and yet so different … I am going to make it. I cannot give in. I have to do this.

Nobody is talking – there are no words to describe the pain, just a muted silence that hangs in the air like the smell of death.

There is no rhythm left to the footsteps.

Jason tries to hum but his throat is dry and it takes too much effort, too much concentration.

Nightfall comes and still they keep on walking.

They have to reach the coast by next sunrise if they have any chance of outmanoeuvring the Germans.

The night sky is ominously silent.

Jason listens hard, but it is difficult to hear beyond the dull ache of exhaustion.

His ears are ringing and he feels light-headed.

There must be planes ready and waiting for them out there somewhere, he thinks, and he cranes his neck up at the spectacular void in the sky and wonders how such a beautiful world can be filled with so much evil.

By sunrise the pain in Jason's feet is too much to bear.

Salt and sand are all that keep him going.

He stops by the roadside to remove his socks. They are sodden, grey and threadbare, smeared with a mixture of fresh blood and sweat.

He tries to force his feet back into his hard army boots.

'Shouldn't have done that, lad,' comes a voice from the line, 'feet will 'ave swelled. Never get 'em back on now.'

Jason grimaces. 'Too small anyway,' he chokes, 'I'll go without.' And he throws them over the hedge into a ditch, continuing along the road barefoot, the fresh air wafting against his feet almost compensating for the sharpness of the gritty stones underfoot. When he reaches the brow of the final hill he momentarily forgets his pain; the sweep of the English Channel, vast and majestic, stretches to the horizon and beyond.

And there he pauses for a moment, suddenly rejuvenated, strangely liberated.

This is it, he thinks excitedly, his feet soothed by a soft carpet of grass. This is it – salvation. We've made it.

PART TWELVE

Tomorrow.

An ink smudge of smoke catches Jason's eye and he strains to see.

The sky is littered black, planes rumble in and out of clouds, there are echoes of gunshot, bombs landing. And before him is the channel, its mighty swell calling him nearer.

Down on the beach are thousands of men, armies of stranded antlike figures in the distance, some lying, others kneeling; their wails of inconceivable pain and despair soaring in volume – rising, always rising – like the temperature, as the sun swathes the beach in its glorious glow.

Jason and the others soon reach the dunes, see for themselves the hundreds of frightened faces, corpses – both living and already dead – groups huddled together, eyes averted from the horrors happening around them.

It all looked so organised, so comfortable from the top of the hill, and now they have set foot on the soft shingle they discover the terrible truth: that death here is only ever a second away and survival is only for the lucky ones.

It's carnage, Jason thinks, nothing but death and despair.

In front of him a horse lies dead on its right flank, bloodied and ripped apart.

And the smell – an unmistakeable stench of decaying life that clogs in Jason's airways and hangs in the air like a putrid perfume, seeping under skin and filtering into lungs.

Bewildered, stumbling in and out of nothingness, he passes a makeshift tent with a red cross daubed on the front. With what the cross is made of Jason does not know – best not to think about it, best not to ask.

There is an acrid smell of antiseptic. Suddenly someone rushes out and almost bowls him over. A man grabs Jason by the shoulders, he is wild-eyed and desperate.

'Sorry, mate,' the man pants, breathlessly, 'looking for the doc, seen him?'

Jason shakes his head, fervently.

'We need him, see? Fractured skull. Bleeding from his ears now. It's not good. Got to get him home, though. For ma – I told her I'd look after him,' and the man rushes off into the reeds, tears streaming down his cheeks, shouting helplessly for the doc.

Jason keeps walking, staying low, instinctively waiting for the hum of planes.

And sometimes the sky does clear for a few moments, giving patches of renewed hope, a heavenly rainbow of unpolluted colour in misty blues and gold, momentarily strengthening the weak and the forgotten and the hopeless.

But then the next one arrives, for they always come back, those droning machines with giant steel wings that eclipse the sun and the beautiful sky, monsters that weave and turn and take aim on their targets with daring precision and merciless brutality.

Jason flops down in a bed of thick reeds to hide.

Other men are already there; two playing cards, a couple smoking cigarettes, nobody saying much. They nod at Jason but that is all.

He wonders if they mind him joining them.

'What are we all doing here?' he asks, breathlessly.

'Nobody tell you? Bloody typical! We're wanted back home to defend the coastline. Got to wait here until someone comes for us.'

'But who's *supposed* to be coming for us? We're bloody sitting targets on this beach. There's only one thing coming our way if we stay here much longer...'

Jason turns his face up to the sky and listens. The other men do the same, silently counting, always counting, until the mighty roar of a bomb landing near the shoreline sends water cascading skywards like an aquamarine firework.

The wait is over. They turn back to their cards.

'Dare say you're right, lad.'

There is rubble everywhere.

With nothing left to say, Jason wriggles away, snake-like, slithering across the grit and grass and rocks to nowhere.

Spiny marshy grass has already been flattened by the thousands of others who have crawled down to the beach in the hope of reaching any sort of sanctuary and by medics dragging old boards, doors, anything they can use as makeshift stretchers for the fallen and mutilated and those who grovel helplessly in the sand.

On the edge of the dunes is a lorry, behind which a new trench has recently been dug out.

Jason half heaves himself, half slides into the trench, stretching his body out, his head resting on grit, legs quivering with exhaustion.

Aching with hunger and fear, he closes his eyes. He knows he shouldn't – every inch of reason pleads with him to stay awake, to stay in control, to keep his senses alert and on guard – but he just can't help it.

Soon the gunshots fade, become so faint that he can no longer hear the anguished cries of pain or the torment of terror-stricken screams. And overhead, the rumble of aeroplanes in the low clouds becomes no more than a soothing lullaby carried on a smoking wind. *Sleep, blessed sleep.*

Hours drift by, darkness comes and goes and still Jason dozes in his deep dark trench of excavated earth.

When he finally does wake – suddenly and with a start, when the hazy morning sun once again breaks through wispy clouds of smog and gunfire, he hears a voice somewhere above him reciting French.

At first Jason thinks he might be in Heaven. Skies are calm and bright, the voice above is soft and reassuring whilst the heat of the sun warms his aching body; no more agonies of war, just the gentle rasp of reeds and seaside gulls circling the shoreline.

But peering up and over the edge of the trench he discovers he is still on the beach. A burial party stands some feet away, backs to him, heads bowed. And there is a coffin next to his trench, a shoddily strewn together casement bound with ropes, ready to be lowered into the grave that has been Jason's bed for the night.

Hastily Jason scrambles out, shuddering, desperate to get away from the death that is everywhere and he crawls away through the grass towards the lorry he saw earlier, coming to rest with his back leaning against the front wheels, the softness of rubber tyres reassuringly warm and giving against his spine.

The beach stretches away in front of him, still swarming with men, some alive, some dying – some already no more than decaying carcasses.

But this part of the dunes is strangely calm and quiet.

He cannot hear any gulls. There is no tension here. All is still. All seems dead.

It doesn't cross Jason's defunct mind to wonder why.

The hunger is getting to him.

He cannot remember when he last had anything to eat.

Straining to open the passenger door of the lorry, he discovers it's jammed; there's a strange acrid smell, but there are lots of strange smells on this beach and he thinks nothing more of it. Besides, there might be something to eat inside.

He has to find out. Fishing his army knife from his jacket pocket Jason begins to hack away at the bolt holding the doors closed. They are heavy, stuck fast, but with some persuasion they eventually creak and swing open.

Instinctively Jason covers his nose, screws up his face, gags. The inside of the lorry is awash with flies, humming, buzzing, feasting on bodies, real human flesh, piled high on top of each other like uneven building blocks, uniformed corpses left to rot: debris of war.

Jason turns and runs.

He's not sure where to.

Adrenalin pulses through his body, directs him towards the beach, to the edge of the dunes where he flops to the ground, out of breath, retching, sinking his fingers into dry fine sand, sobbing tears of misery and despair onto the very place that was to be his salvation.

'You! Up!'

A soldier in German uniform towers over him, a broad muscular boy with a rifle pointing at Jason's head. Jason rises slowly and with an outward show of calm, but his heart is pounding like a loose cannonball in the depths of his quaking chest.

So this is it, he decides, wiping his eyes with the back of his sleeve, gaze fixed on the point of the rifle, sweat forming on the palms of his hands.

I've wondered what it would feel like and now it's really happening. And he pictures the lorry, those corpses.

'Come!' The soldier looks agitated.

Jason feels in his pocket for his knife. He strokes the cool blade and metal handle with shaking hands.

'Come! *Now!*'

A rifle jabs into his side.

'Okay, okay, keep your hair on.'

'Halt den Schnabel, Dummkopf! Shut up, *fool*!'

Jason feels a sudden rush of anger at the German soldier's brutality. Temporarily losing sight of the fragility of his own mortality, he lunges for the gun barrel. But the other man is much bigger than Jason; he launches towards him, sending Jason sprawling to the ground.

With Jason floundering the German soldier gains confidence. Legs astride him, he hammers the shiny butt of his rifle down towards Jason's chest. Jason swings his body first to one side and then to the other, thrusting his arms out in front of him to shield his chest from impact, dodging for his life.

Eventually he manages to grab hold of the rifle, gripping the shiny wooden barrel and wondering, just for a split second, if the other man is as frightened as he is.

The two men roll into the dunes, through the grasses, growling and cursing, their breathing ragged, both grappling for control of the gun.

But then time stops.

Everywhere becomes quiet in an empty space between war and peace.

The German gives a final growl and smashes the gun into Jason's shoulder. Pulling the trigger, his face is contorted with horror, with fear and self-loathing, the blast jerking Jason backwards into the dusty grit.

Seconds later Jason glances up and sees a look on the other man's face – a look of victory – but also of panic and regret. Then Jason feels the searing heat, the sharp burning agony as a bullet embeds in his shoulder and lodges there, between bone and ligament, muscle and tendon.

The German towers over Jason, gun pointing shakily at Jason's heaving chest, and Jason can see his face clearly for the first time; can sense the trepidation with which he handles his weapon, the fear that shrouds the bloody job he has been consigned to do.

Fumbling in his pocket, Jason grasps his knife.

He knows he only has a few seconds. Leaping drunkenly to his feet, he swings viciously, plunging the steel blade into the other soldier's groin before emitting a blood-curdling scream and snatching the knife back out again. He drives the knife repeatedly into the man's flesh, feels it sink deeper and deeper with each thrust of the hilt.

Eventually, in one last surge of defiance, the German soldier reaches out and grabs hold of Jason's jacket, pulling Jason down with him as he slumps to the ground – eyes still open, staring straight at Jason, body flinching.

He twitches once, twice, stiffens and then is still.

Jason collapses on the sand. He grips his injured shoulder tightly. Breathing heavily, he can't swallow properly or steady the drumming in his ribcage.

Blood is seeping through the fibres of his coat, a spreading fan of rich cherry red liquid that drips between his fingers and over the back of his hand, before falling onto the earth in a shallow pool.

The bombs return with their incessant howls, their ear-piercing warnings of death. Sometimes they land close by, when giant puffs of sand are thrown skywards and fall back to earth over the mutilated, like funeral confetti, and sometimes they are further away, whining, droning thuds that scatter and maim.

The German's body is slumped across Jason's legs. Jason wriggles to get comfortable. He is in no hurry to move. He has nowhere to go anyway; and if any more Germans come along he can always pretend to be dead, lying under the body of his victim.

Afternoon turns to evening. The sun sets and the temperature plummets.

Eventually the pain in Jason's shoulder subsides to a steady pulsing throb, but the hunger returns.

There is an inch or two of water in a flask in his bag. It's been there for a few days, but it's better than nothing.

With fading hope of ever getting off the beach alive, Jason wonders if anyone really *is* coming to save them; if all this killing and fear and hopelessness actually have a purpose; if any of it is going to make any *real* difference in the long run.

'I've never killed anybody before,' he mutters out loud. 'God knows I've wanted to … but I've never done it … until now. I thought it would feel good, like a dream come true. I've waited long enough, haven't I? But I don't feel anything – just emptiness.'

He looks down at the face below him, at empty eyes that stare but see nothing.

'It was me or you, I had no choice, mate – I'm sorry – I had to do it.'

A soldier crawls past Jason on his stomach, leaving a line of fresh red blood on the sand like a giant coloured slug trail, his left ankle ripped open by bomb or bullet.

'Dying for a fag,' whispers the soldier weakly, 'got a ciggy, mate?'

Jason shakes his head and the man crawls slowly away into the grasses to expire.

Jason suddenly needs a cigarette, too.

He rummages through the soldier's pockets, just in case.

'You don't need them now,' he murmurs, apologetically, 'shame to waste them.'

But his hand touches something else in the pocket besides cigarettes and he pulls it out. Why not, there's nothing else to do here? It is a brown leather wallet embossed with initials S.B.

Lighting up, he closes his eyes and takes a long draw.

He feels like a thief again, rifling through the tiny compartments in the wallet, a million miles away from guns and smoke filled skies and the overwhelming stench of death that whisper *you could be next ... you could be next ...*

But there are a only few bank notes, photos and some bits of paper with messages scrawled on in the wallet and Jason quickly discovers there is no pleasure in stealing from a dead man.

He picks out a photo of a woman with three small children.

She's pretty, he thinks, turning the photo over.

With all my love, Maria.

Jason's breath catches in his throat.

He stamps the cigarette out on a rock and flicks the generous stub into the long grass.

He shouldn't be looking at this, it doesn't belong to him – it's private, personal.

Jason's mind begins to race, his thoughts adrift on a sea of self-loathing and sympathy. He scrutinises the face of the woman who is smiling back at him so sweetly from the photo.

What will they find in my wallet when I am dead? He traces the outline of the woman's face with his finger. I have no family, no loving wife, no children waiting at home – nobody to miss me.

'I should have died, not you,' he mutters. 'Your reason to live was greater than mine.'

Delving further he finds a letter written on tissue paper signed *meine ganze Liebe, Maria.* It has obviously been looked at often for the folds are paper-thin and barely hold the sheet together. The writing on the body of the letter is indecipherable – German – he can tell that much, and it is addressed to *Stefan Barzel.* Jason looks again at the photo of the woman and her three beautiful children – children who will never see their father again, never feel the warmth of his smile or the reassuring touch of his hand.

The beach is in darkness now save for a few torchlight beams and the remnants of the setting sun. But there is a new gnawing pain in Jason's stomach that clings and chokes, a raw biting emotion he has never felt before that pounds against his chest above the distant hum of war planes. It is not the pain of hunger. It is the pain of love.

Jason stares blankly at the dead man. He sees his jacket stained with the blood of war, hands dirtied with the terror of fighting, blue eyes open, but seeing nothing. 'Stefan Barzel,' whispers Jason. 'Whoever you are I am sorry – so, so sorry. I won't leave you here alone. I promise.' And tears caress Jason's cold numb cheek before dripping down onto the dead man like holy water. Jason begins to sob like a small child, his body racked with a silent convulsion, he weeps grievously for this stranger and for the family who have lost him. Eventually there are no more tears left to fall and Jason reaches down to cradle the dead man, rocking him backwards and forwards as a mother would rock her child, consumed by love, losing the barrage of hatred that has barred the path and plagued his voyage for so long.

Much later, when night is almost turning to dawn and sheaves of light flicker over the horizon, when Jason's eyes are still sore and swollen and his body aching for yet more sleep, there comes a raucous commotion from the shore.

Jason peers towards the sea, every inch of his flesh prickling with an extraordinary desire, a renewed passion, the certainty of his fate suddenly becoming clear. Through the myriad of bodies, men and ammunition, he sees hundreds of boats, all different shapes and sizes, all advancing towards land.

Men are racing down the beach and splashing into the water, leaping above the lapping tide, jumping the waves, shouting and screaming to the boats, waving their arms.

When they reach the boats they clamber aboard, as many as can fit in and sometimes more besides, hulls weighed down with their excessive cargoes.

Then these boats turn and row out to larger ships that can't come into the shallow waters, the men transferring onto bigger ships before the little vessels turn back towards the shore to do it all over again.

'Come on, mate!' shouts a soldier, leaping over the grasses, galloping past Jason and clouting him on the back of the head on the way, 'can you believe they're here? I thought they were never bloody coming! What you waiting for?'

Jason smiles and watches him as he lollops away.

Soon the man who shouted to him reaches the shore with the thousands of others, all swarming towards the boats, tiny ink-dots on the cluttered landscape.

'I knew they would come,' Jason shouts to the soldier, afloat with a strange drunken sway of optimism, '...but there's no rush. I've waited this long, haven't I?'

Another man races by. 'Better get a move on – there ain't enough boats for all of us, mate.'

The scene is strangely reassuring. Jason has seen the boats somewhere before but he can't quite remember where, and a silent voice in his head whispers ...*everything is going to work out just fine... everything is going to work out just fine.*

But it isn't long before heavy bombing begins again and the sky is once more filled with ghostly whinings and rumblings as aeroplanes circle overhead, dropping their loads on the boats and the rolling sea.

Soon the little boats must hurriedly retreat from the shore, whilst on the sand men cry for them to come back, to turn around and rescue them, as bombs continue to land in the bay.

There is an explosion and one of the bigger boats out at sea is hit.

Panic reverberates along the beach like ripples from a spring tide. Some of the smaller vessels go to pick up survivors who cling onto driftwood, trying to stay afloat in the turbulent water.

But soon the sea is quiet again.

Jason puts the wallet back in the dead man's pocket, wriggles out from beneath the corpse and stands up.

He feels dizzy, his shoulder is still bleeding heavily, and he takes a moment or two to gather his breath. Then, in a sweep of selfless courage and without any thought for his own wellbeing, Jason turns to the dead man and picks him up, balancing him across his two forearms, the clogging pain in his shoulder burning like fire.

He carries the dead man like this down onto the beach, the two of them united by death and war, by love and hate.

Jason keeps his eyes fixed firmly on the grey water ahead, but as he reaches the beach, he senses the panic. Men who are too injured to walk, crawl hopelessly towards the shore. Men who can't crawl, lie sobbing, shouting for help, begging for someone to carry them to safety.

Jason cannot hear them – he *won't* hear them, doesn't allow himself to – because he has to do this last thing for the stranger in his arms, for Stefan Barzel.

There is a shout from behind.

'Get down! Get *down!*'

Thudding to the ground, Jason covers the dead man's body with his own and closes his eyes. He tries to take a deep breath in but his lungs won't oblige; fear has taken hold, and pain and panic. He has to make do with short sharp rasps of air that lodge in his throat and barely enable him to function. He keeps his head down, pressed into the gritty earth, the smell of dried blood and death hanging in the air. His mind is everywhere right now, everywhere and nowhere. His senses have taken over, primeval instincts for survival.

He waits.

There is little else he can do but count – five, four, three – a blast jolts the dunes, showering sand over Jason and sending splintering shards of rock cascading into the air.

Jason lifts his head.

He can taste salt and sand and burning wood. It sticks between his grimy teeth; he crunches grit, spits out solid lumps of gravel, wipes shards of glass from his hair.

'Here, sonny, you look done in.' A tanned arm hooks under each armpit and lifts Jason from the earth to his feet.

Jason slumps thankfully against his rescuer for a moment or two, unable to bear his own weight, but then he remembers the dead soldier and the promise he made to him.

'Don't try, sonny.' The man seems to read Jason's mind. 'You'll never manage a dead weight like that. Here, let me.' And the man with tanned arms picks up the soldier and sets off in front of Jason towards the shore.

'Cheers,' whispers Jason weakly, staggering through the sand behind the man, tripping over legs, guns, discarded clothes, avoiding the blank gazes of the dying, desperate not to hear their forlorn pleas.

They reach a jetty.

The man sets the body down gently on the wooden pier in a sitting position, its back resting on paint-peeled planks.

'You'll be fine here, sonny. A boat will come for you.'

'Will it? asks Jason. 'When? We're too late. They've all gone.'

'Have faith,' whispers the man. 'Dream of the boats, sonny, and they will come back. I'm going now. I've not finished yet.'

'But what if they don't come back in time?'

'Dream, sonny, keep dreaming of the boats ...'

And then the man walks away up the beach, leaving Jason nothing but the memory of two steely grey eyes and a selfless resolve for love.

A small ferry arrives.

Jason shouts for the man with the tanned arms to get on board with him but he is nowhere to be seen, so Jason bundles the dead soldier's body onto the back of the boat as best he can and climbs on board himself.

He can't leave Stefan amongst the tall windswept grasses to rot in a solitary forgotten grave, not now he has a name and a family, not now he has seen pictures of his wife and his children. Stefan may have been a stranger to Jason in life but he is becoming real to him in death. He isn't even an enemy anymore – just another victim of bloody war.

War is the enemy, not those fighting it. Jason has heard that somewhere before, but he can't quite remember where; they are merely disconnected words that flit in and out of his head like shooting stars.

He's so tired, so confused.

How can he be expected to remember trivial things that people have said to him, throwaway comments that don't mean anything?

A rush of water laps against the side of the boat and lulls Jason's eyes closed, whilst distant gulls beckon the flotilla of ships back across the sea to England.

In his dream he can smell blood and sand, carried on the salty breeze, then water being pressed gently against his lips; but he is too weak to open his mouth, barely able to swallow.

'This one's nearly had it,' says a faint voice, 'need to get 'im to hospital pronto.'

'Aye. This one's already a goner. Got a Jerry uniform on he has, too. Seems odd to me. Does it seem odd to you, Jack?'

'Aye, but leave 'im. He's no threat to us now,' and then the voices fade, leaving only the sound of water sloshing gently against the sides of the boat, a calm air of tranquillity that surrounds Jason, steadies his restless heart and soothes his soul.

'You're my brother,' Jason whispers, wearily, to the dead soldier, 'and I killed you – but I had to or you would have killed me. And I know somewhere there is a wife who wants you back, who needs to grieve. From the depths of my soul I promise I will not leave you here. I will take you home. It is the one thing I can do for you now. And I am ready to do it, whatever it takes ...'

Jason is absolutely complete when the bomb falls.

The ferry sinks in minutes. The stern cracks and splits in two like the snapping of a dry crisp twig, water filling the lower deck and taking all on board down with it – deep, deep into the depths of the cold crystal sea.

There are no survivors.

Men who waited on the beach day after day, joyous at the sight of the boats coming to save them, now lie anchored amongst clams and mussels and anemones, their bodies twisted and unrecognisable in the darkness.

But they are only empty shells, discarded carcasses that are no longer needed.

Some will have finished their journey here, already lifted to that better place, whilst others will return to earth once again to continue along the pathway in search of sublime proficiency.

Many others survive, thousands of soldiers who return to England and go on to help secure victory for the allies at the end of the war.

Jason is not one of those men.

His war is over.

The voyage is complete and his moment has arrived.

The spirits are expecting Jason as they promised they would be. A place in the Heavenly House awaits him.

And the spirits are very pleased...

Between 27th May and 4th June, 1940, a total of 693 ships (39 destroyers, 36 minesweepers, 77 trawlers, 26 yachts and a variety of other small craft) brought 338,226 people back to Britain from the beaches of Dunkirk. Most of these were members of the British Expeditionary Army.

Searching

The rules are clear.

Soul Spirits only accept complete beings into the Heavenly House.

Only those reaching sublime proficiency in the Six Absolute Emotions during their voyage through earth are granted Emotional Exoneration, for they are Pure Beings and they have truly earned it.

But it is no easy challenge and it may take several attempts before a soul becomes complete.

Emotions can be complex sensations, you see. They are not always compassionate or tolerant, they do not always show love or understanding; they can be mean and selfish, cruel and deceitful; effortlessly grinding a body down, crushing and consuming it, until all that remains is a seemingly futile existence surrounded by a rotting soul.

The first emotions to creep into a human soul are Hate, Envy and Greed. Once their vile corruption is perfected they are most difficult to denounce – for they cling and grasp like poisonous climbing weeds, effortlessly strangling all that is good in their path – but uproot them is what you must do to search out your place in the Heavenly House one day.

And it is true that Sympathy and Fear can also embed themselves deep into an unprepared soul, often taking certain flair to master and overthrow skilfully.

A strong soul is required to deny these Absolutes.

It is Love, the final Absolute and the one pure emotion that must be preserved and cherished if a soul is ever to be considered truly complete.

You see, to the Soul Spirits, Love reigns supreme over all emotions and its presence in an earthly soul should ultimately oust all others.

Unconditional Love – purest Love – comes only with age and experience and wisdom.

If you have lived a full life, striven well, been true to yourself and to others, then Love will find your soul and a place in the Heavenly House will be waiting for you.

Acceptance

Sometimes a young soul, one who perhaps experiences an ill-timed departure from life because of a tragic accident or an incurable disease, must return to earth again to complete its voyage. These souls are most precious to the Soul Spirits and they love them dearly, for young souls have been wrenched from their earthly families, separated from those who could teach them best, their emotional journey halted like a flick of a switch or the click of a finger.

If you are one of these poor souls please do not be afraid, for the cessation of your journey is only temporary and you will most certainly be sent back to earth again to search for your right to an eternal place of rest in the Heavenly House.

Your second coming may be quite different from your first visit, however, for time flits across the skies with little regard for clocks and appointments and other earthly affairs. Have you ever passed someone in the street you think you recognise? For a fleeting moment you see a deceased relative, father, uncle or even a friend you lost touch with many years ago and you may gasp with the likeness of their image. But when you look again you realise you are mistaken – it is just something about the way they smile at you, or the shape of their nose or the twinkle in their eyes – and you can see they do not recognise you anyway. These are souls you once knew who have come back in search of exoneration, for their voyage was not complete when they were first taken.

All this matters little, anyway.

*You are here for one reason and one reason only —
Love.*

*And it is no use looking for a shortcut to the Heavenly
House, either by begging or pleading on your knees for your
own Emotional Exoneration.*

*The spirits have no say — they are only doing their job —
for heaven has the highest standards imaginable.*

It is flawless, you see.